THE SECRET of ANU

The Secret of Anu

R.K. Dogra

authorHOUSE®

AuthorHouse™ UK Ltd.
1663 Liberty Drive
Bloomington, IN 47403 USA
www.authorhouse.co.uk
Phone: 0800.197.4150

© 2013 by R.K.Dogra. All rights reserved.

No part of this book may be reproduced, stored in a retrieval system, or transmitted by any means without the written permission of the author.

Published by AuthorHouse   08/13/2013

ISBN: 978-1-4817-7006-4 (sc)
ISBN: 978-1-4817-7007-1 (e)

Any people depicted in stock imagery provided by Thinkstock are models, and such images are being used for illustrative purposes only. Certain stock imagery © Thinkstock.

This book is printed on acid-free paper.

Because of the dynamic nature of the Internet, any web addresses or links contained in this book may have changed since publication and may no longer be valid. The views expressed in this work are solely those of the author and do not necessarily reflect the views of the publisher, and the publisher hereby disclaims any responsibility for them.

Chapter 1

"Gosh, John, you did a wonderful job with this patient."

"Mary, when there's a question of being human, then the only thing on your mind is the patient's welfare. That poor woman made herself a wreck by pleading with that heartless Indian doctor to operate on her wounded husband. Those lunatics had shot the unsuspecting man three times. He could have bled to death if we hadn't moved just in time and managed to save him."

"I know. That clinic is private. That's why the doctor was adamant that she should pay the fee in advance for the operation before he'd proceed. They should have brought the patient to this hospital in the first place."

John nodded his agreement. "From what I've learned, the victim was working in his bicycle repair shop," he said. "Suddenly, a gunman appeared from the back door of the shop and started firing at the unsuspecting man. The attacker fired three shots and ran off. There were two employees working with him; they stopped the first car coming towards them. The road is usually busy at midday, and some kind person stopped his car. When he saw the man covered in blood and holding on to another person, he quickly drove to the nearest medical facility."

"Right," she said. "Unfortunately, it was a private nursing home and they were told they would have to pay in advance to have an immediate operation. The victim, Mr Oberoi, had an uncle and cousins, but no one was forthcoming to help the unfortunate family. I'm glad someone told Mrs Oberoi to bring her husband here to Mathege Hospital, where it would be easy to get treatment since it's a government hospital. Anyway, I still say this family was lucky to have been brought under your care."

"Sure, but don't forget that the bullets passed just by the heart, damaging his liver. That was the hardest part to deal with. Still, the man had a strong and healthy body, which made the operation successful."

Dr Kimberley had come to Nairobi in 1935, when an epidemic of malaria claimed a vast number of lives. All the missionary doctors were busy treating the unfortunate victims of this deadly disease.

When he had told his sister, the only surviving member of his family, about his decision to go to Africa, she was horrified. "You just can't leave me alone and shoot off to some unknown place, John! You know very well that I promised Mum and Dad to look after you till you got well settled in your career."

Gillian was in her thirties and John only in his late twenties, having just finished his MBBS. He had a vision of doing something worthwhile for humanity. Going to Africa was his main aim. He came to learn that a group of missionary doctors were going to East Africa, most probably to Kenya, where there was a shortage of qualified doctors.

John had been blessed with a healthy body and mind. With his tall frame and well-built body, everyone looked up to him. Maybe his persona was what made him a much-loved member of the team of young doctors who had to stick close with each other throughout the long journey that eventually brought them to the Port of Mombasa, located in Kenya.

He had a special interest in studying tropical illnesses, perhaps because his father had been a doctor and John used to help him whenever he could. His interest had been aroused by his father's dedication in treating the sick, so when it was time for him to make a decision for his future, he chose medicine. Sometime during medical college, he decided to travel abroad.

Just before his graduation, he received the drastic news about the death of his father. He had to come home straight away, and on his arrival, he was shocked to see his dear mother lying in a coma beside her husband's corpse. She never recovered, and within a short space of time, she joined her husband as well. John had wept, clinging to his elder sister. He had never shed a tear in his life, but the sudden realisation of losing his mother and father so soon broke his self-control completely.

That was when he decided to go far away. It would be easy to forget everything and just concentrate on dealing with people who needed him. He'd left not only his sister but also his girlfriend of long standing. He didn't need any commitment of any sort that would make it difficult for him to fulfil his desire.

The new environment and wilderness of Kenya had taken his mind off his worries back at home. At first, he had to go out of Nairobi with a team of doctors who had been called by the big mission hospital based outside Nyeri, a small hilly town about eighty kilometres from Nairobi, the capital city of Kenya. He liked the surrounding hilly area with scattered houses. Most of the local African people lived outside of the town. It was a common practise for the Asians to live within the town centre and the natives to live in small villages. The white community had their bungalows and detached houses at a distance from the Asians and Africans.

As soon as he got accustomed to his surroundings, there was a call for him from Mathege hospital in Nairobi. Malaria victims were increasing in numbers, and there was a shortage of doctors. Therefore, most of the doctors were called back. Dr Kimberley was one of them.

The MO had called him to his office as soon as John arrived. The rest of his team members had dispersed to their appointed living quarters. He was the last one to receive his instructions.

"Well, Dr Kimberley, I have arranged your accommodation in a secluded bungalow on the outskirts of Nairobi. The flats for the hospital staff are all full."

He was glad that there was someone to receive him when he arrived at the new house. A young Kikuyu boy of about fourteen had opened the front door of his new home. "Hello, Bwana Dactari. I am Kamau. I am appointed as a houseboy by the chief medical officer." He had a wide grin on his chubby face. John was surprised that the boy spoke decent English.

"You speak very good English, Kamau," he said, stroking the boy's head softly.

"I worked for an English lady. She taught me how to speak English. She also taught me how to keep the house clean and tidy."

John was relieved that he could carry on his duties at the hospital with a free mind. The only snag was that he still had to eat out. Sometimes he would take a break and have a quick snack at the hospital canteen.

One day Kamau brought a proper cook to ensure that his master could eat healthy food at home. A twenty-two-year-old Indian girl, who looked closer to the age of eighteen, took over the kitchen duties.

This petite young woman impressed John. When he found that she had lost her father in a car accident a few days earlier, he'd felt a great surge of sympathy for her. Inwardly he was glad that Kamau had come to her rescue when she had nowhere to go.

As time passed, he was able to get involved with the local habitants outside hospital duties, which made his early memories of life in England like a distant horizon. He was happy to work amongst the white and Asian doctors. Something about his attitude attracted everyone towards his humorous persona. His comforting words acted like balm to soothe the pain of serious ill patients.

Since coming to Nairobi, John had found a close ally in Mary, who was a junior doctor in the same hospital. It wasn't surprising, because since the very first day John started his duties in the hospital, his dynamic personality attracted Dr Mary Wilson so much that she started finding any excuse to be near him. It wasn't long before she started to invite John to her house. It became a frequent routine for both of them. John knew what was in Mary's mind. He was amused at the thought because he too was lonely. He also needed company, a female one at that. But he didn't want to commit himself to any relationship that might lead him into a matrimonial trap. He wanted to stay free from any permanent commitment.

Mary knew about his wish, and she respected it as well, thinking that there was no harm in getting intimate without any ties.

It was rather late when they emerged from the operating theatre. After completing some formalities with the patient's family, they left for the day. Both were deep in their thoughts while driving towards Mary's house.

"It's very late, John. You'd better come in with me. I will dish up a quick meal. I don't know about you, but I'm starving." Too tired to argue, John relented easily.

Mary had bought a little flat a short distance from the hospital. She also had come with a team of doctors to Nairobi, but unlike John, they were all from Italy and France. Her colleagues had left after one year, but Mary had fallen in love with the place and had declined the chance to go back to specialise as a gynaecologist. She was happy working here, far from home in England. With a broken engagement and a broken heart, she wanted to be far from painful memories and have a carefree life in Nairobi.

Mary had met Gavin, a fellow student, at medical college, where both were studying medicine. All through the course of their studies, they had been inseparable. But on graduation day, he came to see her before the ceremony finished, and taking her hand in his, he had said words she could never forget.

"It's been nice being with you all this time, Mary. Now I have to say goodbye to you, for our paths do not go the same way. I have to go join my parents in Glasgow, where the rest of my family lives. I shall always remember you as my best friend, the one who pushed me to achieve my goal.

"I can proudly stand in front of my father and say, 'Dear Father, look, your son does you proud now by becoming a doctor at last!' Because when I left home, he told me with confidence that I'd never be able to finish even the first year at the university."

Mary had only looked at him, feeling as if she were going to choke, but no words came out. She kept quiet. She didn't even reply to his farewell gesture. She kept looking straight at Gavin's disappearing figure until it was lost somewhere in the distance.

She couldn't digest the fact that all the time they had been together, she had thought he was serious about her. It was difficult to accept the fact that while she had been dreaming of a future with him, he'd never intended to settle anywhere with her. *What a selfish scoundrel he had turned out to be!*

She had hardened her heart after that and vowed never to look at another man again, but seeing John for the first time had broken her resolution. There was a strong attraction, and she could not keep herself away from him.

"I am tired and hungry too, so I will definitely accept your kind offer," John said, looking sideways at Mary and giving her a gentle push.

After making him comfortable on a sofa, she put the music system on. There was a vast selection of records stacked neatly on the bottom shelf of her little wooden cabinet. She loved music, especially soft romantic music.

"Mary, please put on some country music; you know the kind I like." John gave her a pleading look.

She gave him a wide-eyed look, and their gazes locked for a while. When she felt her cheeks getting hot, she immediately lowered her gaze.

"Oh, sure, John. I have a good selection. I still can't believe that the previous owner of this house left this gramophone machine behind, not to mention some furniture. What luck that I can listen to my favourite songs! I love listening to music to soothe my tired soul."

She started shuffling through her prized collection. She was down on her knees, her blond hair falling over her chest. She looked quite appealing and desirable, and John was only human. Mary was an attractive young woman, tall and slender as well. Her blue eyes and pink lips were enough to fill a man with desire. For one moment, he had an urge to gather her in his arms. He was about to reach out to her but stopped when she turned to him excitedly.

"Here's my favourite one, John!" she said excitedly. "Listen to this number; you'll start swooning over this song. I never get tired of listening to this one."

John became so engrossed in the song that he put his head on the back of the settee and got lost in the sheer melody of it.

Mary was feeling some inner excitement. After preparing a quick meal, she got out a bottle of wine and called John over to the romantic atmosphere that she had created for them. It was a quick but fine meal, washed down with splendid wine. John was feeling slightly light in the head.

It was early hours of the morning when John opened his eyes. The sharp rays of the morning sun were cutting through the windows, as if to tell him that it was daytime already. He sat up and saw Mary lying next to him, fast asleep. He suddenly remembered last night, and thinking about it made him smile.

Now with the presence of Miss Lakhani, the Gujrati cook, in the house, he started having regular meals at home. It was rare that he was out at night. He had come to like the change in his house these days. Miss Lakhani also excelled at continental dishes, so John wasn't deprived of his favourite English and Italian dishes. Besides the kitchen duties, the new maid also made the entire house look beautiful. There was a thorough feminine touch everywhere.

He kept his liaison with Mary but only occasionally spent the night with her. He knew she wasn't happy that there were very few nights when they worked late together. He shrugged, realising that he had made it clear to her that they were only friends and nothing more than that.

"Mary, you should not waste your time over something that can never be yours," he'd told her. "There's a big wide world out there, and one day you'll find the right man with whom you'll want to spend the rest of your life."

"Don't worry, John. I am not so desperate for male company that I will fall for any man who comes my way," Mary had replied, her voice full of remorse.

John knew she was a tough woman. She was going to involve herself in her work at the hospital, which would eventually get her over the infatuation she had for him. Relieving his mind of the guilt, he started taking more interest in his work, in his patients, and in his home life.

The housemaid, Miss Lakhani, whom he preferred to address as Ani rather than call her by her long surname, had turned his house into a home. At the end of the day, he was eager to go home. The house looked inviting, with a lovely meal on the dining table. John had started inviting his friends over for dinner every Sunday.

Just when he started to enjoy life in Nairobi, suddenly an offer came his way. One day the MO called him to his office.

He had been watching the young doctor ever since he had appeared in front of him a few years ago. At first, the MO had been surprised that almost all the missionary doctors were nearly middle-aged, apart from a couple in their sixties. Dr John Kimberley was in his thirties; he was very young and had astonishing good looks. He was a little taller than the rest of his co-workers. But the most attractive feature was the smiling expression in his eyes. His sense of humour had made him very popular with the patients and, most of all, the nurses.

The MO was not happy to send John over to Kampala, but the medical association had already picked up John's name from the list of doctors who were eager to go to Uganda. He hadn't known that John had also applied for a job in the Kampala hospital. His face had fallen when he had seen John's name on the list of applicants that another MO had handed to him.

"Ah! Dr Kimberley, take a seat, please." He was going through some notes in a file placed in front of him. John looked at his bowed head, which was partly turning bald.

The MO was short and slightly chubby, and John thought that he looked like *Agatha Christie's Poirot*. He even had the same type of moustache as the detective.

"We had a call from Mengo Hospital in Kampala. They are short of fully experienced doctors. The medical association has recommended you, being a doctor all round. I mean, you are a thorough, experienced doctor, with vast knowledge of working with the natives. Quite a few other doctors also applied for this job, but your name came up as far as being the most suitable person to work in Kampala. So, Dr Kimberley, would you like to take this offer? Keep this in mind, young man: you will have a higher position than here and, of course, a handsome salary as well as all the plus points you will be entitled to."

"What plus points, sir?"

"You will have a car of your own and a comfortable house. There's no hurry for you to give us the answer now. Go home and think about it with a clear mind, and when you come to any conclusion, then you are welcome to come and tell me. I will, of course, wait for your answer to this offer."

John pondered over it for a long time once he was inside the four walls of his house. He would have to let go of this house, which had become like a home now. Sleep evaded him, for his mind was occupied with thoughts and more thoughts—whether to accept the offer or not. Then he accessed the present situation of Nairobi.

He knew that Kenya was under colonial rule, and few people realised that the outbreak of World War II would have a devastating consequence all around them. After debating with his conscience, he made up his mind to accept the MO's offer.

Uganda had been a stable state so far. It would be a nice change, or at least he hoped so. With these thoughts, he left for the hospital. He had done some research on the political situation in Uganda, and he was well satisfied that the step he had taken in his decision to go to Uganda was the right one.

When he returned home in the evening, he went straight to the study room to sort out his papers, passport, and so forth, so he could start packing his belongings. It was a good thing that everything in this house belonged to the hospital authorities. The only possessions he had were his suitcase containing personal items and a trunk full of his medical books, journals, and some personal files. He had also brought some valuable old ornaments from England, and he wrapped them up and placed them on top. He had some sentimental memories from these ornaments, for they had belonged to his parents. No matter how much one runs away from memories, the shadow always follows.

One evening the maid brought a jug of water and a bottle of whisky. She looked at him while pouring the drink in the glass, thinking he looked worried. Handing him the glass, she asked him, "Dr Sahib, you look worried. Is everything okay at the hospital?"

John looked up, and his eyes met hers. For a moment, he thought he saw some sort of longing in them. He had always given her a formal look whenever she was around.

But this time, he looked more deeply in her eyes. For a moment, the light brown colour of her beautiful eyes held his gaze. He suddenly became more aware of her looks, which he had evaded all this time. At the back of his mind, he knew that she was an attractive girl, slim with an oval face and long black hair which she kept tied at the nape of her neck. Her lovely skin was a light corn colour, and she had sharp Indian features. What was fascinating about her whole being was her aura. Whenever she came near him, he felt strong vibes pulling him towards her. He had to put up a great resistance to stay away from her.

He wanted to tell her about his new job but decided to tell her later. But in the morning, he just told her that he might be late coming home.

When he came home, it was nearly midnight. He was feeling exhausted. As soon as he came inside, he found Miss Lakhani asleep in the lounge. When he woke her, she explained to him that Kamau had to go home. His mother was ill. She had promised him that she wouldn't go to her quarters and leave the house empty. She would wait for the doctor to come home in case he needed something.

He was glad that she was waiting for him because it was a good time to tell her about his new job. When eventually he told her, saying that he would be leaving in a few days' time, her reaction had surprised him.

That night had left an impact on John's mind. What had happened that night was so unexpected and sudden that he had sat quietly for a long time, trying to digest the aftermath effect of it. He knew it was baseless to ponder over what he reckoned had been a passing phase in his life.

He left Nairobi at the end of August 1939. When he arrived in Kampala, he was busy in his present post at Mengo Hospital when the first news of the war reached him. He was uneasy about leaving Nairobi behind, as some deep-rooted memories were haunting him more now that there could be trouble with the allies bombing Kenya as well.

Miss Lakhani's memory was making him restless, but he knew that there was no way he could reach her now. He didn't have any information regarding her whereabouts in Nairobi. He only hoped that she'd found a good family to work for and had settled somewhere there. When she had come to bid him farewell, he had handed her a large envelope. She had hesitated to accept it at first, but when he had looked at her with compassion in his eyes, she did so.

"Accept this little gift, my dear, for your services. It will help you get settled somewhere in the midst of Nairobi, where there are lots of Indians who have come from the Indian subcontinent. Lots of them have their own businesses, and hopefully you will be able to find some sort of job with one of them. This money will pay for your board and lodging until you find a secure job."

He had slipped into the envelope a note with his address at the hospital in Kampala. He had hoped to hear from her. Eventually, with the passing of time, the memory of her mostly faded.

In the early 1940s, the British government realised that they needed to recognise the nationalist feelings in the country; and by the mid-1940s, steps had been made to promote African advancement in the civil service and for political office. Africans were appointed to the legislative council in Uganda in 1945.

Social change was taking place at a quick pace in Uganda during the 1940s. At the beginning of the decade, the colonial state was a caste society wherein caste decided both social and economic positions. The Europeans controlled most of the administrative and businesses, and the Asians were shopkeepers and traders. Some of them were white-collar workers in the government and private sectors, both Indian and European. There was a small section of high-class Africans, but the majority of Africans preferred to live in the countryside.

The missionaries brought the political transformation by educating the lower classes of the society. This undermined the stability and stirred up sensitivity about social inequality.

Dr Kimberley stayed in Kampala for five years. In January 1945, there were labour riots in the capital city. He decided to move up North. He chose to work in the mission hospital on the outskirts of Gulu.

Before he could go to Gulu, there was an urgent message from his sister. There was some property dispute regarding their ancestral home, based on the outskirts of Maidenhead, near London. So Dr Kimberley started to pack for a long journey to England.

When he came back to Uganda, he was a fully qualified eye surgeon as well. He had made good use of his free time in England. He had realised that his job in Gulu was going to be of greater responsibility than before. As the job was going to be in a missionary hospital, he knew that the local natives of the region would get free treatment. He had mastered the Swahili language, and he was sure to learn more of the local dialects in the Acholi and Lango districts of the province.

John had made some more enquiries about the mission hospital in Gulu. The earlier missionaries who were working in Sudan had to abandon Omach, on the eastern bank of the Victoria Nile, because of sleeping sickness. Under Father Antonio Vignato, the mission post was moved to Gulu in 1938. Besides the cathedral, the missionaries also founded some of Uganda's finest hospitals, including Lacor in Gulu and St Joseph's in Kitgum. Lacor and Kalongo had nursing and midwifery schools attached.

Gulu District was bordered by Lamwo District to the north. It was the capital of the Acholi sub-region. Here at last, he felt at home. The local people were mostly of the Acholi and Lango tribes. It took him only a short period of time to get settled there, and within a year, he had married Carol. She was a senior nurse and was a midwife as well. He was enjoying his hospital life and domestic bliss, and he had mingled with the Asian community of Gulu rather well.

After Uganda got its independence in 1962, things seemed settled in Uganda. Or at least that was what John thought, as he was far from the politics of the country. There was some restlessness among the high-ranking people who were part of the political parties. The unexpected happened in the middle of the night in April 1966. The kabaka's palace was taken over by Obote's men, and the king had to flee the country.

As Obote was from Acholi District, there wasn't much bloodshed there. Things were different in and around Kampala, though. Dr Kimberley was glad that there were not many casualties in Gulu, because there was a shortage of doctors in the hospital at that time.

There were few doctors working in the hospital, and apart from him, there was no other specialist to assist him in emergency cases that eventually had to be referred to Mulago Hospital in Kampala.

One day he was sitting in his office, going through the post he had just received. The medical association was sending a team of doctors who had done their internship at the Aga Khan Hospital in Nairobi. He glanced through the names on the list. There were three African names, one European, and one Indian. He smiled when he read the name Dr Vickram Patel, for there were already a number of doctors with the name Patel, who had private practices in Gulu.

He felt relieved that now he could take some time off to spend with Carol. Lately he had been working late at night dealing with emergency cases long after Carol went home after finishing her work for the day.

"Carol, we're going to have some more doctors to help with emergency cases at Lacor," John told Carol as she was making a cup of tea for him. "At the moment, there are three doctors coming from Mulago Hospital. They were supposed to go back to Nairobi, but the MO over there offered them another job so they could gain more experience working with the local people of Northern Uganda."

"I'm glad for you, John. You'll be able to have some free time at the weekends. I know you've been feeling guilty when I'm alone."

Carol had met John soon after he had come from England. Both of them were attending to a delicate case of a pregnant woman. The complication of the case had made her ask for the help of a doctor. It was very late at night, and luckily Dr Kimberley was around at that time.

The senior midwife, Caroline White, had big help from John in delivering a baby that night. The young couple beamed with happiness, as this was their first baby after several years of marriage. After that incident, Carol started looking at John with adulation. She never had looked at any man twice before. It wasn't in her nature to have any emotional attachment with men.

It took several months before John could muster up the courage to propose to Carol. In due time, they moved to a bigger house, located outside Gulu town. The only snag in their otherwise blissful life was a lack of children's laughter in the house. John knew that Carol had longed for a child of their own, but as they had married late, maybe that was the cause of her not being able to conceive a baby.

As time passed, she'd became very busy with her work at the hospital and had little time to think about anything else. However, the weekends were long for her. She was feeling happy that John would be at home more now.

Chapter 2

Vickram hadn't thought that he'd be leaving Kampala without finding any answer to his query. Even after spending almost eighteen months there, he was nowhere near finding the truth about his mother's secret. He had tried his best to dig up any information from almost all the medical journals of the hospitals in Kampala. Disappointed, he finally he made up his mind to return home.

Before he could think about packing his belongings, there was a change in the political scenario of Uganda. Mulago Hospital had to send some more doctors up north of Uganda. Idi Amin Dada had taken power as president of Uganda and was mercilessly killing the local Acholi and Langi tribal people. Vickram changed his mind about going back to Nairobi and decided to join the team of doctors who were going to the mission hospital near Gulu.

Arriving in Gulu, he liked the look of the place and quickly found a place to stay. As he began to unpack in his flat at the end of the high street of Gulu, his eyes caught sight of a framed picture that was lying upside down on the top of his clothes. He picked it up, and after wiping dust off it, he put it on the bedside cabinet.

It was a beautiful picture of a young girl dressed in a long dress that was in fashion in the thirties and forties. Her black hair was tied behind the nape of her neck, half covered with a printed scarf. For a long time, Vickram looked at the picture with compassion. There were unshed tears in his eyes.

His mind went far away, to that fateful night that had toppled his world over completely, ensuring that life was never the same again—not for him at least!

Mr Girish Patel's phone rang. He had been sitting near it ever since he had returned after admitting his sick wife to the hospital. He could have taken her to the big government hospital in Nairobi, but he wanted his wife to get the best treatment. Therefore, it had to be a private clinic.

He did not inform his son about this clinic, knowing very well that as a doctor, Vickram would have insisted on admitting her to the same hospital where he was working. He was surprised when Anuradha had refused to tell Vickram about the seriousness of her condition.

A few years ago, when Vickram had just gone away to study medicine, his mother had started to lose weight. Mr Girish had noticed that slowly her health was deteriorating.

After some check-ups, their GP prescribed some vitamins and advised her to watch her diet. Since the birth of the twins, Anu had been under the weather most of the time. She never regained her previous vitality to enjoy life to the fullest.

Vickram was back at home now as a fully qualified doctor after graduating with a degree in MBBS. He was lucky to get a place at the Aga Khan Hospital to do a year's internship. As it was his first year there, he had to stay within the hospital due to the late shifts. Vickram loved little children and had a desire to specialise as a paediatrician in the near future. The MO of the hospital knew about Vickram's passion for small children, so he had appointed his duties in the children's ward.

Vickrim also wanted to spend some time with his parents, especially his ailing mother. He was aware of her mother's weak health and was keeping a constant watch on her by phoning home or going over to see her whenever he could get some free time.

It would have been easy for Girish to phone Vickram, but he couldn't do so. He wanted to be sure of his wife's condition before notifying his son. After a thorough check-up, Anu was diagnosed as having a problem with her ovaries. All those years when she had been complaining about that pain she was having, nothing had been done. It could be due to the lack of medical knowledge during that time; perhaps the doctors couldn't pinpoint the real cause of the problem. If Anu had been monitoring her health properly, then something could have been done when she experienced the earliest symptoms.

When eventually Vickram was notified, the doctors told him that their diagnosis did point at the possibility of the ovaries being affected, but even the most experienced gynaecologist couldn't analyse how serious the problem could be without operating. Vickram and Girish were in favour, so the doctor started preparing for surgery.

Vickram had to leave in order to attend an urgent case at the hospital. Before doing so, he asked his father to phone him as soon as his mother was going to the operating theatre. But alas, they had to postpone the idea, as there was a sudden change in Anu's condition. Her belly swelled up suddenly, alarming the doctor. They were afraid of this, for it was a sure sign of cancer going beyond control. The doctor told Girish, "I'm sorry, Mr Patel, but we can't operate in this condition."

Girish was told that his wife had very little time, but they couldn't tell him how much. He had arranged for the best medical care that the hospital could provide. He sat down next to Anu's bed, holding her hand.

"Anu, my dear, can I call Vickram now? Look, at your request, I haven't told him about what the doctor said. But please let me call him now."

Anu's eyes had sunk in and looked lifeless. She turned her gaze upwards and closed her eyes tightly, her voice low as she whispered, "As you wish, Girish. Go ahead and call him."

The receptionist at the Aga Khan Hospital picked up the phone. It was quite late. She took the urgent message and passed on the message to the duty nurse of the children's ward. She was told about the urgency of the message, so she raced towards the children's medical ward.

She saw the doctor checking the pulse of the little boy.

"Well, master Kirit! You seem to be doing very well. Your temperature is back to normal now." Vickram was reading the thermometer he had just taken from the boy's mouth. The boy, named Kirit, looked adoringly at Vickram, as if this doctor had just given him his life back.

The little boy had had a constant high fever. After a routine check-up by the family's GP, Kirit was admitted to the hospital a few days earlier. The GP couldn't find the cause of the high temperature, which didn't seem to come down even after the right medication was administered.

Vickram was able to diagnose the real cause: a severe infection of the ear, even though there was no sign of any pain there. A course of antibiotics was prescribed, and with close monitoring, the fever left as the course of antibiotics ended.

Today the final trace of the fever was gone. After a solid two weeks, Kirit was looking well and ready to go home. Suddenly, someone came rushing towards him. He looked up and saw one of the nurses. Before he could say anything, she burst out.

"Dr Patel, there's a call from your father. He wants you to go straight to the nursing home where your mother has been admitted."

"Thanks, I'll go straight away." He told the ward sister to take over Kirit's case, as he had to go out urgently. Explaining about his mother's serious condition, he dashed off.

When he arrived at the nursing home, the receptionist told him that his mother had been taken to the ICU. He couldn't believe it; it was only on Sunday when he was with her! She looked fine except that she had lost a lot of weight in the last couple of weeks.

With quick strides, he was outside the ICU room. He turned the handle and slowly opened the door to go in. An icy chill went down his spine at the sight of his dear mother lying helpless on the bed. Her eyes were closed due to heavy sedation. His eyes misted over, and quickly wiping the unshed tears, he was beside her bed in a quick stride.

Nobody could believe that this ailing frail woman had been a glowing healthy woman only a short while ago. Vickram was shocked to see her in this state of bad health, for since he had gone to the UK, he had hardly been in touch with his parents. All he could remember was the sadness in her eyes when he had said bye to her before going away. He never realised that he had spent such a long time away from home.

Since coming back after graduating, he had seen some sort of contentment on her face. He was glad to see her like this, so he had decided to come and see her regularly in his off-duty hours. He had been home for a couple of months when his father had told him about his mother's illness.

"Papa, why didn't you tell me about this before? I should have been with you to look after her!"

"I know, son, but you know your mama! She has this habit of concealing her inner feelings. She'll bear the pain but will never let anyone even guess that she is hurting. You know, Vickram, when you left home to study medicine in the UK, I started noticing some change coming over her. I thought maybe it was the changing hormones; you know, the midlife crisis all women go through! But I never realised that there was any serious problem until it was too late. You know the rest, my son."

Girish looked haggard and tired. He seemed to have lost any hope of Anu's recovery. He knew that she had only a little time left, but even in his wildest dreams, he hadn't expected the end to come so soon. He got up and went to stand at the foot of the bed, staring at the still figure of his wife.

Girish was thinking of the time when Anu had appeared in his life like a ray of sunshine.

Girish Patel was one of the early settlers who had come from India in search of better prospects for a secure future. His father had had been one of Mahatma Gandhi's ardent followers until he was shot by the British force during one of the peaceful marches led by Gandhi.

Girish had become disheartened by the turmoil in their daily life. He made up his mind to go abroad and start life afresh. Luckily, one of his close relatives was in Kenya. Mr Praful Patel was happy to help him.

He had studied accountancy while he had been in his hometown of Ahmadabad in Gujrat. Praful Patel had no difficulty in getting a good job for him with the railway authorities. But Girish was a man full of ambition. He wanted to be somebody—a successful businessman if possible. Therefore, with the help of Praful, he set up a wholesale business in grains and spices that were exported from India. Eventually, by the time he was in his early thirties, his Midas touch had made him one of the wealthiest businessmen in Kenya.

He had built a comfortable life in Nairobi by building a huge bungalow on the outskirts of the city. Slowly a number of houses owned by the rich began to appear in the neighbourhood. It was strange that most of the rich and successful businesspeople preferred to live away from the busy life of Nairobi. The middle-class community occupied the centre of the rapidly growing city. They had their shops in the congested part of Nairobi. As most of the schools and the religious places were situated within the centre of the main city, a majority of the people preferred to live near these accessible venues.

As soon as the house was built, Girish decided to call over his widowed mother and his young sister from India. Their life changed from a struggle back in India to a more comfortable one in Nairobi. His mother, whom he affectionately called 'Ba', started to hint about getting a daughter-in-law. She wanted to see him happily settled while she was still around.

Girish was in a dilemma. How could he tell his mother that he was quite old for any eligible girl to marry him! Ba had been busy looking around as well, hoping that a suitable bride would turn up one day for her son.

It happened unexpectedly. Ba was delighted when one day Girish brought home an attractive young girl. He introduced her as the new housekeeper.

"You know, Ba, Anuradha is a Gujrati. When I found out that her father had died recently, I decided to offer her a job in our house. She wouldn't have come here otherwise, so offering her a job was the alternative at the time. Her pride would be saved if she earned her living. That's why when I came to know that she was looking for a job, I immediately offered her the job of a housekeeper. She had been working, and for some reason, she left the employment, saying that it was far from the town. Besides, she could be a good companion for you, Ba. You can gossip in your native tongue as much as possible."

Anuradha eventually became a part of the Patel family. One day, he told Ba that he had decided to marry Anuradha. As Girish's sister had left Nairobi after her marriage, the house had looked barren, but after Anuradha's arrival, life had started to look beautiful to Ba.

Ba was content with life in general after she became a proud grandmother of a bouncing baby boy. With the birth of twins, she had the fortune of seeing another addition in the family. She doted on her daughter-in-law, whom she affectionately called Anu. Gradually, everyone started calling her by this name.

Unfortunately, Ba didn't live to see her grandson Vickram graduate to become a doctor. The little girl, Puja, and her twin brother, Akash, were there to keep Anu busy. Life kept moving at a steady pace—until the day that everything just turned upside down.

Girish had never expected that life could be so cruel to him that when he needed his wife by his side, to spend the rest of their lives together, fate would decide to snatch his lifeline from him.

As he was away from home most of the time, his children had depended a lot on their mother. He never realised how suddenly the twins had become their teens. When Vickram had gone away for his studies, Puja and Akash had been with their mother. He wished that he had spent more time with her in the absence of Vickram. He was regretting the missed moments when he took his wife's presence for granted. It's only when those precious moments are gone that the true value of those moments begins to surface.

I wish there were some way to put the clock back! His heart was crying out, but he kept his mouth shut. All he could do now was watch the emotional scene between a son and a mother.

He had seen Vickram pull the chair closer to his mother and lift her frail and wrinkled hands, lying listless on her chest. He placed them on his eyes and sobbed. "Mama, please get well quickly. We are very lonely without you!" He placed the cold hands back on her chest and buried his face on her still form. He felt some movement in her hands and then felt them stroking his hair. He didn't see that her eyes had opened a little.

But Girish had. He saw her gaze moving towards the door. He understood her gesture, and moving towards the door, he looked back at his wife. "I'm going to call the nurse," he said, closing the door behind him.

Anu's hands suddenly became active, and she tried to pull Vickram's head up so that she could see him more clearly. He sat up, and his heart gave a jump. His mama looked better!

"Oh, Mama, please get well quickly! Our family is not complete without you. You are the pillar of strength for all of us. We can't see you like this, Mama!"

Anu put out her shaking hand to stop him from talking. Vickram saw that she had pulled off her oxygen mask and was trying to mumble something. He moved his ear closer to her mouth to listen clearly to what she was trying to say. She was clearly trying hard not to mumble.

"Vickram . . . my son . . . please f . . . or . . . give me. . . . I . . ."

"Mama, what are you trying to say? Please put the mask back on!" He was horrified to see that her eyes had closed again; she wasn't saying anything either.

She was breathing fast. Vickram tried to put the oxygen mask back on her mouth, but she stopped him. She was whispering now, and he could barely make out the words.

"Girish . . . not . . . your father."

There was a sudden jerk from Vickram. His mouth opened, but he couldn't say anything. How could his mother say that Girish Patel was not his father? But then he realised that a dying person wouldn't tell a lie. He took hold of her hands, and bringing them to his face, he looked pleadingly at his mother.

"Then who is my father?" His eyes had fear in them. He was dreading hearing what his mother was going to disclose now, if she would be able to. She must tell him the truth. He must make her talk!

At this moment, Vickram felt that he was standing on a clifftop. Ahead was a vast sea and stormy waves to engulf him if he slipped, but behind him, there was a wild animal also waiting for its prey.

If he ignored what his mother was trying to tell him, he would be committing suicide deliberately, and if he came to know the truth, then he would have a struggle ahead to face. He chose the latter and moved his face nearer to hear clearly what his mother was mumbling now.

"Your . . . real. . . . father . . ." She seemed to have great difficulty forming the words. Her eyes flickered for a little while, looking straight in Vickram's eyes. There was a smile playing around her almost sunken lips. Then her eyes closed, her lips moving to utter her last words before her face fell to one side.

"He . . . was . . . a . . . doctor, Eng . . . lish. Went aw . . . ay to Kam . . . pala." She whispered the words that were barely audible, but Vickram heard them all right. When he saw his mother's face, he let out a strangled cry.

"Mama!" He grabbed the lifeless body of his dear mother and tried to shake her, thinking she would respond.

By now, Girish had come into the room, followed by the doctor, who looked at the still figure on the bed. After checking her pulse and her eyes, he declared Anu dead.

There was a deathlike silence in the room. Vickram lifted his tear-stained face and saw his father looking silently at the still figure lying there. He felt a surge of compassion for this dear man he had always known to be his father. Slowly he got up and went towards the unfortunate father, who couldn't even cry, but the grief and pain were clearly visible in his eyes.

The shock of losing his mother was bad enough, but knowing about his actual identity was like a catastrophe that engulfed his whole being. His heart was crying out that his mother hadn't told him the name of the doctor. How could he find out about this nameless person?

Anu had breathed her last, and with her confession, she had left a big wound in her son's heart.

There was one person who could have comforted him at this time. That was his grandmother, whom he lovingly called 'Ba', but she had died when he was away in England.

For the first few weeks, he was like a zombie, a lifeless robot going on with his daily life, drained of any emotion. His father got worried and had a good talk with him.

"Life goes on, Vickram. This is the nature's way; life and death is in the hands of our creator.

You are a big strong man, and you also have to look after your younger sister, as I am away most of the time. I wish Akash were here, but it's his first year at the university, and I didn't want him disturbed in the midst of his exams."

"But, Papa, he should know about Mama! Otherwise, he will never forgive us if he finds out from somebody else."

"Leave that to me, Vickram. I will inform him later, as he will be asleep at this time." He looked at his watch. It was not even eleven o'clock in the morning. His younger son, Akash, was at Boston University, working toward his MBA.

Girish Patel was happy that at least his one son was interested in business. He had encouraged Akash that if he wanted to succeed in this field, then he should acquire an academic achievement. That way, the business would reach sky high.

Puja was only three minutes younger than Akash. Being a twin, he still preferred to refer to himself as Puja's elder brother. Whenever he had tried to bully her, she had run to Vickram. It was obvious that for her, the elder brother was like a hero in every aspect.

It was bliss for Puja and Girish to have Vickram near them, especially now, when they were feeling grief-stricken with the loss of their mother. On the other hand, they were not unaware of the turmoil that had engulfed Vickram. They knew how close he was to his mother, and she had also treated him with special care. It was her wish for Vickram to become a doctor. Not that he had to oblige his mother, for he'd already made up his mind during his school days that he wanted to do something in the medical field.

"I think you're right, Papa. I will resume my duties at the hospital as soon as possible." Vickram hugged his father, who heaved a deep breath of relief.

After Anu's death, there was a melancholy air around the house. Puja seemed to have gone back in her shell of self-isolation. She was like this when Ba, their grandmother, had died.

She was only ten years old then, and Ba was always great company for her. Afterwards, she had clung to her mother so much that Girish used to get worried about his daughter's insecure state of mind.

Vickram was worried about leaving her alone in the house. On the other hand, he had to go back to the hospital as well. So after having a talk with his father, he went to Puja's room.

She was sitting on a chair and looking out of the window. An open book was on her lap but turned upside down. He went over to stand beside his sister's still figure. Becoming aware of someone near her, she turned her face to see her brother standing behind her.

"Vickram, my dear brother, you startled me!" She tried to get up, but Vickram made her stay seated.

"Don't get up, Puja. I just came to see you regarding your plan to study further. Papa just told me that one of your applications to study graphic arts has been accepted. Congratulations! I'm glad that you will have a goal to work for now."

"Thanks, brother, but I will be going away far from home! The university is in Nainital, India."

"Not a bad choice, Puja. At least you won't get homesick with our own people. I'm referring to Indians, with whom you could get mixed up easily. It wasn't easy for me when I was in the UK. It took me quite a while to adjust to the English people and their lifestyle. I was homesick for a long time. That's why I am glad you're going to India. We could have sent you to America, but then we would have been worried about your being in an alien country."

"I understand your concern! I didn't want to go that far as well. But still, you'll allow me to come back for the summer holidays at least?"

Vickram smiled and hugged her with affection, telling her that her wish would be fulfilled.

With Puja's worry out of his mind, he settled in his daily routine at the hospital. One day there was an urgent call for

• The Secret of Anu •

him while he was on duty. He came quickly to the reception desk and picked up the phone. He had been waiting for this call for quite a while.

"Hello, Vickram. I'm sorry that it took me a long time to collect all the information you asked me to get from the medical journal of the hospital, but I have it now."

"That's good news, Satish. Look, let's meet somewhere for lunch. I think Dinu's Lunch Box will be an appropriate place. It's near the hospital and is a bit far for you, but you do have a car to drive you straight there. Meet you there at exactly twelve thirty."

For the past months since his mother's death, Vickram had been busy making inquiries about all English doctors who had worked in the hospitals before the wartime. It was difficult for him to get access to the medical journals that were in the government hospitals.

Aga Khan Hospital was a private one. With a busy schedule of work, he couldn't get away to visit other hospitals.

Satish was his friend from his school days, and he was working at the King George VI Hospital. It was a short distance from the town centre. Both of them had chosen the medical profession, but now they were working separately. Still they kept in touch.

Dinu's Lunch Box was a posh restaurant situated near the main road going towards the city park. The restaurant was a convenient place for tourists who were sightseeing, especially going to see the park.

Vickram was the first to arrive, and he quickly found a place in a corner. There was a small table with two chairs.

Satish joined him just as the waiter was approaching them. They shook hands, and after giving order to the waiter, they took their seats.

After having a hasty lunch, Satish sat up straight. He put his empty glass of water back on the table and turned towards Vickram.

"Well, Vickram, I know you are anxious to know the outcome of my research. While searching the medical journal, I also came upon some old records from a very old hospital. I don't think that hospital is in existence now. I think it was called Mathenge. That hospital must have been closed. By chance, I spotted a handful of stained yellowish papers tucked inside the cover sleeve of the journal. When I tried to pull one paper out, the whole lot fell out. When I picked one up, I saw the name Mathenge Hospital written at the top. I couldn't wait, and putting the thick copy of the journal back, I sat down on one side and started looking through each paper.

"Then I saw the names of some doctors who had gone to Uganda before the war. There was an English doctor who had left sometime in nineteen thirty-nine. The name was hardly visible due to the faded ink. There was one name with words missing. I couldn't find out about his address in Kampala because there were four other doctors who had also gone to Uganda besides him. But he was the only English doctor; the others were Italian and Indian."

"What about these other doctors? If we could find out something about them, then we could trace the English doctor easily." Vickram's voice had a trace of desperation in it. "There must have been some mention of the hospital in Kampala. At least the medical journals in those hospitals could throw some light on this matter?"

"No, Vickram, there was no mention of any hospital in Kampala. Anyway, it all happened a long time ago. Tracing somebody without a name would be like looking for light in a dark tunnel." He got up to go, and before he reached the exit door, he suddenly stopped and turned back. "I'm wondering why you are so interested in this anonymous doctor!"

"I'm sorry, Satish, for giving you so much trouble, but I cannot disclose the reason that I am looking for this person. Anyway, thanks a lot. At least you have given me a lead that the doctor who left Nairobi in nineteen thirty-nine went to Kampala. I'll always remember your kind gesture, and I will definitely let you know if I happen to find anything about him."

He was feeling uneasy for not telling Satish the reason he was looking for this doctor. It was his mother's secret which she had kept within herself all her life. He did not intend to break her trust.

After his meeting with Satish, he decided to come home. He wanted to see his father. There was something brewing within him that was making him restless. He wanted to say his piece and then start to put his plan into action.

After supper, his father went into the living room and switched the television on. He was watching and listening to the news attentively. The latest news was about the sudden exodus of all those people who had British passports. They were given a deadline to take advantage of going to England before the time came when they'd have to apply for a visa to enter Britain. Shortly after, when Girish turned the television off, he noticed that Vickram was standing near him.

"When did you come in the room, Vickram?"

"When you were busy watching the box," Vickram replied, looking at his father affectionately. He came and sat down next to him.

Girish looked up at him with a question in his eyes. He knew that his son had been restless ever since Anu's demise. After a long pause, Vickram found his voice.

"I wanted to ask you something, Papa, but not here. I don't want Puja to hear what I have to say. My room will be appropriate, I think."

"No problem, Vickram. You go to your room. I'll be there in a couple of minutes." Girish smiled.

It was late at night when father and son came out of Vickram's room. Girish stopped outside the door and turned towards his son. "I understand your decision, Vickram, to accept the new post at Mulago Hospital in Kampala. Truly speaking, I was hoping that you might settle here in Nairobi and proceed with your medical practice. I could have helped you in starting your own clinic, but what matters is what you want. You want to go to Uganda, go! You want to see the world before settling down, no problem. Actually, I think you will be fine in Uganda. Things are not so good since Kenya got its independence.

"There are always ugly incidents taking place within Nairobi. The thefts and murders of innocent Indians have increased. I can never understand this hunger for power. The African leaders have been so eager to grab the power of leadership that once finding that power is there for them to exploit, they sit in bewilderment afterwards, when they realise that they have a very difficult task facing them. The mismanagement of economy has made the common man pine for his basic needs. So they start stealing and sometimes kill their victims. That is why most of our Asian friends have left to go back to India or go to Britain."

"I'm glad that Puja has opted to go to India for her studies. But I am not happy to leave you alone here, Papa."

"I'm fine, my son. The business keeps me occupied. You know that since your mother died, my widowed sister has moved from Mombasa to stay near us. If need be, I'll ask her to come and stay with me."

Vickram knew about Sarla Auntie. She was a lovely person, just like Ba. He could see that his father was trying to put on a brave face, but his eyes had a haunted look in them. He didn't want to leave his father, but the circumstances had made him harden his control over his feelings. He had no choice but to pursue his quest.

Puja was upset to see him go away again but tried to bring a smile on her face while she bade farewell to him with his promise that he'd keep in touch by phoning them regularly.

His father had been following the latest news regarding the political situation in Uganda.

He knew that after toppling Edward Mutesa from power, Obote was in charge of running the country with the help of his army chief. In July 1967, Obote had created the military police force under Major General Idi Amin Dada's command. In turn, Amin recruited forces from his home region of West Nile among Lugbara. Girish Patel heaved a sigh of relief that Vickram wouldn't have to face any problems while in Uganda. The political situation was well under control now.

CHAPTER 3

The new job at Mulago Hospital was quite satisfying for Vickram. He didn't want anyone even to guess that he was there for any purpose other than his duty as a doctor. For the first few weeks, he just lost himself in his work. He loved little children, and there was no shortage of ailing infants and sick children.

Two other doctors had come with him from Nairobi. They'd found a nice place to live, and it was only a few minutes' walk from the hospital. As they were there only for a short while, they preferred to stay in this guest house that belonged to an elderly widow by the name of Esther DeSouza.

She was an English woman who had married a Portuguese businessman and come to Kampala in 1930. Her husband was much older than she and had died a few years earlier. He had left behind a prosperous business and a big house, which was too big for her. She had decided to turn it into a guest house, keeping only a portion of it for herself.

Martin was her only son, and he took care of looking after the business and the house. He had moved to another house when he got married, but he never missed his daily visits to see his mother.

He came to see how the new guests were getting on in the new place. There were two of them sitting in the lounge reading the daily newspaper and having a cup of tea. He greeted them warmly and sat down next to them.

"Well, I'm glad that Mother will have the company of you young doctors while you are staying in our guest house. I must say that she always has the pleasure of having student doctors as her lodgers. You're the first ones who are not students. I believe all of you have jobs at Mulago Hospital. I hope you are well settled here. Kampala must look very different from Nairobi, right?"

Vickram had looked up from the paper, and now he smiled at Martin. "Actually, I think this place looks much more peaceful than Nairobi. I mean, there is less traffic compared to the busy roads of Nairobi. I think we will enjoy working at Mulago Hospital. We're lucky to have the company of your mother. She reminds me so much of my late grandmother."

"I'm glad to see that you have adjusted very well in this environment. It's taken a lot of worry off my mind now that she will have young company again. The previous lodgers were also young. There were two girls sharing a room and three young men in the other two rooms. They were students from Makerere College, and once their studies were finished, they left. Mama gets miserable in the empty house." He got up to go, but Vickram stopped him.

"Why don't you join us at the breakfast table, Mr DeSouza? As it is Sunday today, I'm sure your mother will be delighted to have your company more than ours."

Martin looked at his watch and then looked at Vickram. "I'm going to phone my wife and will then come join you." He went in the landing hall, where the phone was kept.

Esther was waiting for them. The table was set for three. Vickram pulled out his chair and smiled at the elderly woman. "We're having one more person for breakfast, madam!" Before she could ask about that person, Martin walked in.

"It is only me, your son, Mama!" He laughed and went over to hug his mother. "I phoned Jenny to let her know that I will be spending the morning here. Also, I didn't have enough time to get to know our new guests. It will be nice to have a good chat after breakfast in the lounge. What do you say, young man?" He was looking at Vickram before turning towards the others.

They agreed with his suggestion, as they were not planning to go out before the evening. Vickram was thinking that as Mr DeSouza was years older than his wife, then it was obvious that he must have known a lot of doctors who were working in Kampala in the forties and fifties.

He got his chance to talk to her when Martin left and both of the other doctors went to their rooms. Vickram sat there until they were no longer within earshot, then he turned to the older woman.

"I was waiting for them to go, madam. Do you mind if I take a little more of your time? I want to ask you some questions that have been bothering me." Vickram took his chair close to her.

"Don't hesitate, my dear. Go ahead and ask me anything. I'll try to help you. I have noticed that you are different from the others. They're here to work only, but you have a faraway look in your eyes even when you are talking to others."

Vickram told her a sob story about a friend of his who was trying to find his father. The only person who would have the answer was a certain English doctor. When this friend learned that he was going to Kampala, he begged him to try to find this doctor. He must be in his sixties now.

"The problem was that he couldn't tell me the description of this doctor except that he had come from Nairobi sometime in nineteen thirty-nine. I'm also trying to find out from the hospital records, but I was also thinking that maybe your husband could have mentioned some good doctors when he was working in his shop. Deepak's Pharmacy is only a stone's throw from the old hospital in Kampala. I think most of the doctors recommend your pharmacy to their patients."

"I agree with you, my dear. Let me think for a moment." She was quiet for some time, gazing at the floor.

"I remember that there were quite a few doctors at the old Kampala hospital. My husband was always talking about an Indian doctor, a kind human being because he used to give free treatment to those who were poor or disabled and unable to work. And I think there were two more doctors working with him at that time."

"Can you remember their names, madam? I am more interested in the English doctor."

"Sorry, Vickram, it was long time ago. I have forgotten their names. We always used to refer to them as our English doctor or Indian doctor and so forth. I wish I could have helped you more. I'm sorry."

Vickram caught her hands and tried to speak casually. "Don't be sorry. I can still ask around. Anyway, I enjoyed talking to you, madam."

One day there was a call from Satish, his old buddy from Nairobi. "Hello, Vickram! I have some good news for you. My sister got married last month to a doctor working in that old hospital in Kampala where the English doctor used to work in the early fifties."

"That's great, Satish! Is there any chance of meeting your sister's husband?"

"Sure, Vickram."

That day, Vickram finished his duty at the hospital and rushed home. His landlady was surprised to see him come home earlier than usual, and before she could say a word to him, Vickram was out of the house like a whirlwind.

It didn't take him long to find the house. He knew the way to the old hospital that was situated in the heart of Kampala. It was a shantytown called Kiseni, a thickly populated area compared to the rest of this grand city. He managed to get hold of Dr Varun, brother-in-law of Satish.

He took Vickram to the registrar's office at the hospital. Luckily, the office was empty. Varun pulled out a chair for Vickram to sit on while he got busy with the files. The filing cabinet looked very old, and it was difficult to read the faded labels. Countless old files had been lying in the cabinet for God knew how long.

"Here is one file that has the details of an English doctor who came here from Nairobi in nineteen thirty-nine. His name was Dr J. Nicholas. The last name is not visible due to dampness or water spilling over the page. The wording looks like one blue patch. The first name is slightly readable, though the *N* is also faded but readable."

Varun handed Vickram the open file. The information indeed was correct. He wanted to know what happened to the doctor. There must be some more information about this! He flipped through the pages in a frenzy, but all he could find out was that the doctor had left in 1951 and gone back to England.

Vickram's blood started to boil. He banged his fist on the desk. "Damn! I was so near the truth yet still so far from it!"

Varun looked at Vickram, feeling sorry for him. He had noticed that this information was important to him. He took the file from Vickram and put it back in the drawer.

They came out of the hospital, and before going back, Varun said to Vickram, "I want to ask you one question, Vickram. Will you go back to Nairobi now?"

Vickram was quiet for a while. Then he nodded his head. "I'll go back because I have my family waiting for me over there."

"Actually, Vickram, if you want to gain some more experience in your profession, then you could go to the Northern Province, mainly occupied by Acholies and Langis. There is a mission hospital in Lacor, which is only a few kilometres from the main town of Gulu. There's a shortage of doctors there. Think about this seriously, Vickram. It will mean giving full justice to your profession. If you want to take up the challenge, then have a talk with the MO."

It wasn't easy to leave his work at Mulago Hospital because he hadn't even done one year yet. Moreover, more than anything, he was interested in carrying out his practice as a doctor. Realising his first duty as a doctor, he lost himself in his work.

During this time, there were rumours that Obote's hold on the general public was becoming weaker. As always, the root cause was the economic situation of the country. The people of Uganda were getting a bit wary of this president. The common man was still struggling to make ends meet in the daily needs of his life.

Towards the end of 1970, the MO of Mulago Hospital called Vickram to his office. "Well, Dr Patel, you've been here for almost eighteen months, and I hope you have gained enough knowledge and experience. Now the time has come to give you a break and allow you to move on. Are you interested in going up North?"

"It seems that I am destined to move up North!" Vickram gave a chuckle. Picking up his portfolio folder from the desk, he looked at the front cover and then started to scratch the back of his head. Frowning, he looked at the MO, who was already watching him closely.

"Dr Patel, I have a good friend by the name of John Kimberley. He is the senior registrar at Lacor Hospital, the mission hospital about four kilometres from Gulu. He has asked me to help him sort out the shortage of doctors at that hospital. That's why I called you."

"Sir, I had been thinking about exploring the Northern Province of Uganda. But because I had to finish my contract here, I couldn't do anything about it. Anyway, now that I am free to leave this place, I shall certainly accept your offer."

"Oh, by the way, Dr Patel, I forgot to tell you that there will be two more doctors travelling with you as well. Are you surprised? Your buddies from Aga Khan Hospital! They didn't want to go back to Nairobi yet, so are you happy now that you will have familiar faces in an alien place?"

"Thank you, sir. I'm glad that I won't be travelling alone." Vickram shook hands with the MO and took his leave. He was thinking that destiny was pulling him towards Gulu town.

They made a great team of doctors, looking forward to more challenges in their profession, and they started their journey in the morning. The other doctors travelling with Vickram were Dr Mathias and Dr Karim Khan; the latter was a jolly fellow, always cracking jokes, even in serious situations. In reality, he had to endure a lot of heartbreak before he was able to take control of himself and decide to leave Nairobi. He had only told Vickram briefly about the reason for wanting to get out of the place.

Dr Mathias had no family except his old grandfather back at home in Nairobi. His parents had been killed in their village when Mathias was a little boy of five years of age. As he was from a Kikuyu family, his grandfather got help from the government to send Mathias to study abroad, for he was an extremely bright student. He made his grandfather proud by fulfilling his dream of seeing Mathias as a doctor.

Vickram looked out the car window at the scenery, thinking about going to see Murchison Falls sometime when he was well settled there.

The car stopped after crossing the bridge on River Karuma. The driver, Timothy, got out and pointed at a signboard that read Chobi Lodge. As they all got out of the car, the driver asked if they wanted to have a little rest and eat at the hotel.

Vickram looked at his watch. "I think we will be late if we stop here. Don't worry about us. We have straightened our legs, and we do have water bottles in the car. Our landlady kindly packed some sandwiches in case we got hungry."

The air was getting hot. They couldn't open the car windows for fear of dust getting in their eyes. Still, the driver kept his window open a little bit to let some air get to them. The passing cars and trucks left a trail of dust like a whirlwind on the horizon so that nothing was visible for kilometres.

"Do you think that Amin will think of improving the roads at least? I bet he is going to play around with all the wealth left in the coffers now. God save the common men now and help them build up their lives somehow." Timothy heaved a deep sigh. His passengers had nodded off.

Vickram opened his eyes and realised that they had stopped outside a little shack. It was actually a roadside cafeteria that served cold drinks and snacks, mostly for the natives. Vickram saw piles of yellowish bread rolls and packets of lentil savouries neatly arranged on top of the counter. There were crates of Coke and Fanta in glass bottles.

Timothy had already gone to get some drinks for them and was back within a few minutes.

"I know you have water in the car, but due to hot weather, it will have turned warm. These are cold drinks out of the shop's refrigerator."

They were glad to have the cold drink now that they had realised how hot it could get in the afternoon. They thanked Timothy and handed him the money to pay the shopkeeper. But he refused, saying that he already had paid for the drinks.

It was sheer bliss to sit in the open and enjoy the cold drinks with a cool breeze around them. Before they could put their bottles away, they heard some sort of commotion at the back of the shop. The next minute, a crowd gathered there. Vickram was surprised because a while ago, there wasn't a soul in sight. As soon as there is disruption somewhere, people appear out of nowhere.

Timothy found out from the old shopkeeper that his grandson had fallen from a ladder at the back of the shop, used to put the goods on the high shelves. Timothy also told them that the old man had told the boy to avoid the ladder. But children always do what they have been forbidden to do.

It was natural for Vickram to go and see to the injured child. Poor boy! He was lying face downwards with a bloodstained face. He gently turned the boy over and was horrified to see a deep gash above the forehead. The hair was all sticky with blood that was still gushing rapidly from the wound.

Without losing any more time, Vickram asked the other doctors to get his bag from the car. Timothy helped him take the injured boy inside the shop. A space on the floor was made for him, and he had a mat to lie on.

Treating grown-up individuals was no problem for Vickram, but when it came to a child—any child in fact—then Vickram used to forget the time and place and just concentrate on the little victim. He felt that children are the future of humanity and should be protected by any means. He felt sad to see that these natives had to lead such troublesome lives. There was no discipline or any control over the naughty children.

He was glad to see that after cleaning and applying bandage on the wound, the little boy was smiling. The old man looked with adulation at Vickram and kept on thanking him repeatedly. Vickram was glad that the man could talk in fluent Swahili language, for it made communication easier for him. After packing his case, he turned to the old man, handing him some extra dressing and painkillers. He gave him some valuable advice regarding his grandson.

"Remember that a good education is vitally important for these little ones. Send him to a school so he becomes a responsible human being." He took the old man aside and gave him cash to get the boy admitted in a school. The old man clutched the money with gratitude.

After reminding them to keep the bandage clean, Vickram went towards the waiting car. It was getting dusky now, although the sun still beamed at them with its orange and red glow. What a beautiful sight it was! With these thoughts, he rested his head on the back of the seat. They were near Gulu now.

Vickram came to Lacor Hospital when Obote was still in power. Life seemed to be going just the same way as before. The only difference was that in Gulu, it was extremely hot most of the time, while the weather in Kampala was similar to that of Nairobi. All those cardigans and jumpers he had brought from Nairobi were tucked at the bottom of the drawers.

It was a strange place after the busy life in Kampala. Gulu was such a small town that there was no need to take a car if one wanted to explore the place. Some of the GPs lived in the centre of the town, and it was no trouble to visit them occasionally. One of the doctors at the hospital had already arranged for his and the other two doctors' accommodations.

The other doctors working at Lacor had their houses outside Gulu town. There was a vacant three-bedroom flat in the town. It was slightly out of the crowded centre of town. When Vickram saw the flat, he was pleased to see that there was enough room for all three of them to stay comfortably.

The shrilling sound of the doorbell brought him back to the present. He realised that as he was looking at his mother's picture, his mind had wandered away. He put the picture back on the little bedside cabinet and went to open the door. His friends were back.

Lacor was a bit far, and the flat he was sharing with his fellow doctors was in the town. It was sheer luck that he had come across a notice outside an office window. A three-bedroom flat was available. He learned that the owner was a solicitor. The board on the front of the building read aggarwal and co. solicitors. Mr Aggarwal had his offices there but lived elsewhere. Vickram was glad that the office was closed in the evening by the time he came home. There was not much noise to disturb him. He loved solitude, and both Dr Karim and Dr Mathias used to do night shifts on alternate weeks.

After he had been there for some time, he'd gradually started getting to know the people around him. The first person was Dr Kimberley. His wife, Carol, seemed to have formed a great liking for this young man, and she often invited him over.

Today he was alone in the flat. His mates were either doing their late duty at the hospital or were busy entertaining their female friends. Vickram had a lot on his mind and never had any inclination of getting involved with anyone at this time.

The only thought that never left his mind was getting any information he could about the doctors who had worked before him at the municipal hospital and at Lacor as well. He had a gut feeling that one of these days he might come across some sort of clue leading to the identity of the mysterious doctor.

• The Secret of Anu •

He knew that he had to get to know the local people of Gulu town, and being a doctor, there was a great chance of doing just that.

He had been in Gulu for some time now, and apart from going to the hospital, he hadn't done much else. There were no buses in this town, so the hospital had arranged a car and a driver to take him to the hospital every morning. There was always somebody at the hospital to give him a lift back home.

As it was Saturday, he decided to take a stroll and explore this town which looked so small compared to Nairobi and Kampala—just like a village. He wanted to find out if there was a car showroom where he could buy a decent car.

It was a good thing that he lived in the centre of the town, therefore making it easier to find what he was looking for. He was observing the houses and shops on what looked like a busy street. He decided to go into a confectionary shop. Having a little chat would help him to learn something about this place.

An elderly man was sitting behind the counter and seemed to be reading a newspaper. Noticing someone coming into the shop, he quickly put the paper aside. "You look new here, sir! Can I help you?"

"Yes, *kaka*, I am new here. I'm working at Lacor Hospital. I wanted to look around and meet the people of this town."

"You called me *kaka*! Are you Gujrati as well?" He gave Vickram a scrutinised look. His eyes lit up when Vickram

57

replied that he was indeed one. The old man started chatting nineteen to the dozen. This was what Vickram wanted. He found out about a couple of big businesses: a supermarket and a bakery. There were also a big construction business and a big garage on the other side of the town. This was what he was looking for. After getting the information regarding the garage, Vickram took off, and in just a few minutes, he was within the outer gate of Batra Automobiles.

With long strides, he was inside the premises, and he made his way towards the office which was at one end of the workshop yard. Mr Batra himself greeted Vickram warmly. He was a big man, a Punjabi from the look of him. He was going grey at the temples. The roughly kept beard needed a good shave. Maybe his work as a mechanic left little time for him to pay attention to his appearance.

"You are lucky, young man. Only yesterday the car dealers delivered some new cars. I am sure you'll find one to your liking." Saying this, Mr Batra took him to the car showroom in the front of the building.

"We have only a few of these cars, but if you want any other model, we can arrange it to be delivered from our main agents in Kampala." Mr Batra was eagerly showing him a brand-new Peugeot car. It was a white saloon. There were some Volkswagen models as well, but Vickram had made up his mind. He stroked the bonnet of the Peugeot.

"I like this one, Mr Batra. So can we make a deal?"

After that day, there was nothing to hold Vickram back from driving all around the town. He loved to go for long drives, especially towards the airport. He had also found a good place to chill out after a hectic day at the hospital. At that time, Acholi Inn was the only restaurant/inn for the people of Gulu and the surrounding towns. It provided good facilities for everybody.

Vickram was happy to have the company of his mates. Both doctors—Dr Karim Khan and Dr Mathias—had also adjusted to the new environment.

Chapter 4

Friday afternoon usually brought a crowd to this lovely place, a small restaurant called the Acholi Inn. It was a few kilometres away from the town and on the opposite side of Lacor. Most of the young couples were either sitting inside at the bar or having refreshments outside on the patio. In fact, it was the only place at that time where it was possible to relax as well as be entertained. In other words, just to chill out.

Two young girls were sitting at a table at the far end of the patio, sipping cold drinks. "Tanya, why have you called me here? You could have come over to my house. Mama normally has a nap at this time, and we could have had a chat in peace."

Tanya looked at her friend Manjit, studying her for a moment. "I wanted to share my inner thoughts with you, Manjit. I didn't want anyone else to get slightest inclination of what I wanted to say only to you. Even the walls have ears!"

Manjit laughed at her friend's childish remark. "Go on. I'm listening. There's no one to hear what you have to say, and the walls of the inn are far away from us." When she saw that her friend's mind had wandered off again, Manjit prompted her again to speak.

Tanya had a smile playing at the corners of her mouth. "Manjit, you don't know what happened last week! When I came from your house, instead of going straight home, I decided to come here instead. I had just realised that my uncle and aunt were going over to see some friends in Kampala. They wouldn't be back before nine or ten o'clock at night. I was feeling funny—can't explain to you why.

"I was sipping my drink when suddenly my attention was caught by a little boy of about five years old. He was crying as if in great pain and was pressing his stomach with both hands. His young mother was trying to comfort him while looking around to see if she could get some help. I was about to get up, but someone else came out of nowhere and lifted the little boy up in his arms. He looked at the mother while comforting the boy. I heard him telling the mother that the boy was in exceptional pain and he was sure he had acute appendicitis. So it was best if he could be taken to the hospital immediately.

"He asked the boy's mother to follow him, as he was going straight to Lacor. The frightened woman quickly picked up her bag and raced after the stranger. They had to pass by me to reach the side entrance where the cars were parked. When he came near, I couldn't control my curiosity.

"'That was a quick diagnosis!' I said. 'You're not a doctor, and only a doctor could have done that.'

"'You bet!' The stranger gave me such a look that I just shut up.

"I felt really embarrassed when I heard someone say, 'My dear, that man is a doctor. That's why it was easy to diagnose the problem.' I saw an elderly gentleman sitting at the next table. He must have heard me. My God, Manjit, I was so embarrassed! But then I realised that there was no one else to see me humiliated like that. Anyway, I sat there for a long time, just daydreaming about the stranger. Something about him was pulling my heartstrings towards him.

"You know, Manjit, I have never seen such a good-looking man before. I know your Bobby is a damn handsome man, but this doctor was so attractive, in spite of a stern expression on his face."

Tanya stopped talking, waiting for Manjit's comment. There wasn't any. She was quiet for some time. Manjit remained quiet as well. She sighed and continued talking.

"Well, I thought he looked so different from other men. I mean, he looked like a movie star, like Gregory Peck!"

Manjit started laughing. "Tanya, I bet Gregory Peck must be your favourite actor, and it's easy to compare anyone with him whether he deserves the comparison or not. Anyway,

Bobby mentioned that some doctor has recently joined Dr Kimberley's team of doctors at Lacor Hospital. I bet he's the same man. Look, my dear Tanya, if you are really taken by this doctor, the best bet would be to start making frequent visits to Dr Kimberley's house."

Tanya jumped up and went over to Manjit's side, giving her a kiss on the cheek. "You are a real friend. Thanks a lot for coming here. You'd better make a move before your ma-in-law sends a search party looking for you!"

Laughingly they shook hands, and Manjit quickly made her exit. Tanya watched her receding back, and coming back to her seat, she sat there thinking for quite some time. She was puzzled at this sudden change within her whole being. Why was she feeling so restless these days! Even her nights were troubled with floating visions that would turn into a familiar face. She'd never had any interest in any of the young men who had come into her life during her college days. Here in this small community, every person was a familiar one, and she was content with her life so far. But now her world seemed to have changed entirely.

Deepak and Ranjana were neighbours of Dr Kimberley's. They had a small flat in town. When Deepak came to live in Gulu, he managed to get a good bargain on a shop with a two-bedroom flat upstairs. Deepak's Pharmacy was the only one in Gulu at that time. Being a pharmacist, he had come to know Dr Kimberley and slowly had formed a close friendship with the doctor household.

Deepak had decided to move to a bigger house when he realised that he'd need some open space for his niece to play. Dr Kimberley helped him buy the one next door to him when the previous owner, a retired doctor from India, went back home.

Ranjana had a serious miscarriage soon after they came to live in Gulu. It wasn't long before the bitter truth hit them, after going through several tests, that she would never be able to have another child.

That's when Tanya came into their lives—after her parents died in a car crash in Nairobi. Tanya was Deepak's sister's daughter. When Deepak had looked at Tanya for the first time, he felt as if his sister were looking at him. She was the living image of her mother, especially her eyes, which were made more attractive by the light shade of greenish and yellow tinge of colour. Deepak always called her his little kitten because of her eyes.

As she grew, she became more and more attached to Carol and John. Ranjana didn't mind because it gave her more time to spend at the shop, which was getting busier by the day. Carol was happy to have Tanya with her, especially when going shopping. Mr Hassanali and his two brothers were the sole owners of the one supermarket in town as well as a bakery next door. When Carol had taken Tanya to do some shopping for the first time, Mr Hassanali had approached them and looked at little Tanya and then at Carol.

"Hello, Mrs Kimberley. You've never brought your lovely daughter here before." He looked a bit sheepish when Tanya started to laugh.

Carol couldn't help smiling as well, and she said to the bewildered man, "I haven't brought her here before because she only came to Gulu recently." Then she told him that Tanya was Deepak's niece and was here for good. Carol was pleased when he remarked that nobody would believe that Tanya wasn't her daughter. The only difference was Tanya's dark curls, whereas Carol was a blonde.

As she grew up, she became a part of the Kimberley household. There wasn't a day when Carol didn't see Tanya. So when the time came for Tanya to go to Kampala to study further, Carol was devastated. With the young girl around her, she had forgotten her ache for a child of her own. Somehow, she hardened her heart and got herself deeply involved with her already demanding job.

Tanya had come back to Gulu after three years, with an LLB degree. She was glad that she could help her uncle and aunt financially by getting a steady job somewhere near home. She was lucky to get a job with Mr Aggarwal's law firm. Most of her old school friends had dispersed, and she had started to feel lonely. She wanted to share her thoughts with someone with whom she could click.

It happened suddenly one day while shopping in a draper's shop. She met Manjit. There were quite a few textile showrooms and a couple of drapery shops on the high street in Gulu. Tanya used to buy dress material from one of the shops. Manjit was coming out of the shop, and when she saw Tanya standing outside the shop window looking at some dresses on display, she stopped in her tracks.

• The Secret of Anu •

"Nice material." When Tanya turned, she saw Manjit smiling at her. That was the beginning of a friendship that became staunch as time passed. They started meeting at each other's houses or sometimes at the Acholi Inn whenever they wanted to have a good chat.

Manjit was the daughter-in-law of Mr Dalip Singh, who had come to Gulu in the early fifties. His youngest son, Bobby, was a qualified engineer, and Manjit was married to him. Dalip Singh's eldest son was a doctor and a surgeon as well, but he had decided to settle in the UK after marrying an English girl. His middle son also had gone abroad and never returned home. He had decided to make Canada his permanent home.

Dalip Singh was content with life with his son Bobby, who was happy living in Gulu with his parents.

After seeing Manjit yesterday, Tanya was getting impatient to go to the Kimberley house.

She was curious to find out something about this handsome doctor. She was wondering why she hadn't seen him before. Gulu had a very small community, and everyone knew everybody else.

"Hello, Tanya!" her aunt greeted when she arrived. "Where have you been these past weeks? You must have been doing some overtime in the absence of Mr Aggarwal."

"Sorry, Aunt, I have been too lazy lately to go out, and no, I wouldn't do any overtime for that miser! Anyway, the only time I've been out has been with Manjit, and that was yesterday. Last weekend I was home catching on some pending work which Uncle Deepak had given me to do. Today I thought I'd better come and see you, Aunt Carol."

Carol smiled. Everybody knew about Mr Aggarwal and his stingy habit with money. The man wouldn't let his clients hold back even a penny of his fees, but he had a difficult time letting go of even a penny from his pocket. It was true that he had asked Tanya to stay a bit late to complete the work in hand—but without any negotiation about overtime payment. Tanya knew this and refused to budge.

Tanya had come in the kitchen, where she knew Aunt Carol would be busy cooking something nice.

They chatted for a while and had everything under control by the time Dr Kimberley's car drove through the gate. There was another car following his. That meant someone was coming for dinner, as she had anticipated by noticing the special care that Aunt Carol was putting in her cooking today.

"Come on, Tanya. Please help me get the drinks tray ready. Then we'll go join the men outside. They will be seated comfortably by now on the deck chairs."

Tanya went out to serve the drinks, followed by Carol, who took a seat next to John after greeting him and the young man, their guest for the evening. She looked up at Tanya, who seemed to have frozen on her feet.

• The Secret of Anu •

"Tanya, come and meet our guest, Dr Vickram Patel from Nairobi." Carol was about to tell Vickram about Tanya when she caught both of them staring at one another.

Tanya was staring open-mouthed at the handsome man, who was scrutinising her with a narrowed gaze. Time stood still for her, and her whole being seemed to have turned into a statue. She wished the earth could open up to swallow her due to her embarrassment!

John and Carol were watching them quietly. Seeing the confusion in their eyes, Vickram explained the incident of the Acholi Inn. They laughed at seeing Tanya cornered like this.

Soon after, they were all having tea with Carol's home-made cake. Tanya was about to take a bite when she caught sight of a white Mercedes coming through the main gate.

Dr Kimberley got up to welcome Mr Hassanali as he got out of the car. Someone else was also getting out. Shaking his hand, Dr Kimberley greeted him and saw that Hassanali's brothers were also with him.

"Good afternoon, Doctor. It seems I picked a wrong time to come. You have company."

"Welcome, Mr Hassanali. It's nice to see you after a long time. Meet our new addition to the hospital staff of Lacor." John introduced the new doctor to him. "This is Dr Vickram Patel from Nairobi-Kenya. Anyway, come and join us for a cup of tea. Very traditional way of entertaining our guests—a cup of tea! You could be feeling hot and could do with a glass of something cold to drink."

Hassanali laughed. He accepted the offer of tea for himself and for his brothers as well. "There's something I wanted to discuss with you, Doctor. My brothers, Karim and Amir, have a plan: we should start making use of the tennis court you had built at the back of your house. Just the other day, we realised that we spend all day serving customers. When we get home, there is the family waiting to go out, either to the Acholi Inn or for a long drive."

Karim completed the explanation. "That's why we thought that there should be some sort of activity to keep us fit and also relax our tired minds after a hectic day."

"Not a bad idea; our women could join in as well. What I was thinking, Hassan, is that you could join me playing golf since we both love the game. The rest of you could start playing tennis. I have no objection."

Tanya jumped up with excitement. "I don't believe it, Uncle! At last we can have some activity in our otherwise boring lives. I shall get Manjit and Bobby to join us. It's funny that only the other day, Aunt Carol was telling me that you and your previous neighbours used to play tennis regularly every Sunday."

"You're right, Tanya. We do need some activity in our lives. I have seen Hassanali's wife a few times in town while out shopping. She has her sister come stay with her. I suggest we start next Sunday. You can inform Manjit and Bobby as well."

Tanya had been watching Vickram from the corner of her eyes. He had been listening to them quietly, but afterwards he also joined them in making plans for the next Sunday.

"It would be nice to join you girls in playing tennis. I am not one who has patience to play golf."

John smiled, and turning towards Vickram, he said, "Well, young man, you and Bobby are welcome to join these ladies. I think Hassanali and his brothers are champions at playing golf. I'll gladly join them."

It became a routine for them to meet outside the tennis court behind John and Carol's house.

Carol played hostess by serving tea and biscuits afterwards. But their joy was short-lived.

One Sunday, Hassanali's brother Amir had a game opposite Bobby. Somehow the match became quite fierce, as both excelled at the game. All of a sudden, when Amir lifted his racquet to catch the ball, his body twisted and he lay there on the ground like a sack of potatoes.

Vickram was the first one to grab hold of Amir when his big body hit the ground. Seeing that he was unconscious, Bobby helped him put Amir in the car and rush him to the hospital.

"What a horrible end to one of the most enjoyable days!" Tanya was staring open-mouthed at the cloud of dust left by the speeding car.

"We should notify Mr Hassanali and John immediately, Tanya!" Carol said, rushing over to phone the manager of the golf club, asking someone to give the message to Dr Kimberley.

Monday morning brought upsetting news for all of them, especially for Amir, who had suffered a serious stroke. His left side had been affected.

"He should not have played tennis at all!" John said.

Carol tried to defend Amir. "Why not, John? He is young and healthy. I know he's put on a lot of weight lately, but that's why he wanted to do some exercise—to get rid of the bulge on his midriff."

John was still adamant about his view and tried to tell her the real reason of his concern.

"I agree that exercise is good for keeping fit and slim, but Carol, the man had high blood pressure. He had been warned earlier on not to take part in any activity that could get his pressure soaring so much that he could suffer a stroke!" There was a painful expression on his face when he said slowly that the tragedy of this accident was that at the tender age of thirty-five years, he was going to be invalid for life.

After Amir's accident, no one ever played tennis again, not in that tennis court at least. It was painful for them even to mention the word tennis!

• THE SECRET OF ANU •

After this incident, Tanya and Vickram often met at the Kimberley house. Every Saturday, Tanya used to make an excuse to go over to see Aunt Carol. She knew that Vickram was definitely going to come with Dr Kimberley after finishing their duties at the hospital. After helping Carol make tea for all of them, they would sit out on the patio, enjoying their siesta. Sometimes Vickram would ask Tanya to accompany him to a movie in Kampala, and sometimes they'd just spend time together at the Acholi Inn.

Tanya had this feeling that Vickram was keeping something to himself. Whenever they were close to one another, she noticed that his eyes never met hers directly. Once or twice, she had caught some sort of pain lurking in those mysterious eyes.

She was sad that even after being together for nearly a year, she still didn't know what made him tick. One thing was clear as far as she was concerned: she loved Vickram deeply. She was prepared to wait for him to declare his feelings one day. For the time being, she wanted to spend as much time as possible in his company.

CHAPTER 5

Amin took over Uganda on 25 January 1971. He took advantage of the turmoil within the army. The sudden takeover of the power of running the country had left everyone speechless. Since Obote had taken over the reins of ruling over Ugandan people, the country hadn't prospered much. There was an uneasiness and hostility amongst the army chiefs. In fact, the head of the army was Idi Amin Dada. Obote himself relied too much on this bigger-than-life army general.

Dr Kimberley was troubled by some unforeseen calamity. The country was going through financial crisis. Obote seemed to have lost his magic touch of bringing stability to Uganda.

There were people working in the government services who were giving news of the latest development in the trade and commerce of the country. The news wasn't good, but he hadn't expected the storm to engulf them so soon.

One day Obote had gone to a neighbouring country for a conference. He wouldn't have dreamed that his most trustworthy general would stab him in the back. Obote had to find a refuge where he was staying at that time.

There was great rejoicing and celebrations all around Uganda. When Obote had taken the power reins from Mutesa the kabaka in 1966, the public didn't celebrate his victory. But now, with Idi Amin Dada as their leader, there was a furore in the country. No one had seen so much jubilation in the country, especially in Kampala.

Things were not so promising for the people of the Northern Region, especially around the Acholi region. As Obote was from the Acholi region, Amin went on a killing spree of these innocent Acholi people.

Gulu was the town centre where many killings took place. There were mostly Indian people within the town centre, but as the local Acholi natives lived in the fields, their homes were scattered all around the Gulu town. Amin didn't spare them.

There were dead bodies lying in the streets of the town. This rampage went on for days and days.

There were some Indians with thriving businesses in Gulu. They had to shut their workshops and offices for many days. There were still some unpleasant scenes to be witnessed by most people of the town. All Indians living around Gulu had stopped going for picnics outside the town. Chobe Lodge became deserted now that no one came to spend the weekends there. The Karuma River used to be the main attraction for everybody. Now people travelling to and from Kampala saw dead bodies floating in the water.

Every day there were numerous victims being admitted in the hospitals. The municipal hospital in the centre of Gulu swarmed with casualties. But the most horrific scenes were outside the town. Most of the natives of Acholi origin lived in the huts that were in the middle of the cultivated fields. They were easy prey for the bloodthirsty devils of Amin's army.

It was a hot day, and Dr Kimberley had been attending to these patients non-stop. There were half a dozen doctors working beside him. All of a sudden, the double doors of the casualty ward were thrown open. Before anyone could say anything, a number of guns were thrust towards the doctors.

"We are here to see that no Acholi should survive. You doctors will treat them and make them well again. We won't allow that to happen!" one of the soldiers snarled, and the next moment there was a shower of bullets and then the heartbreaking screams of the dying victims.

Everything happened so suddenly that within minutes, the terrifying sound of the marching boots vanished.

Dr Kimberley was staring ahead, his hands outstretched towards the dead bodies lying on the beds. After the commotion, everyone was stunned by the shock of what had happened.

Somebody came towards Dr Kimberley and gently caught both of his hands. "It's okay, sir. They have gone." He put his arm around the senior doctor's shoulders and slowly walked him towards the reception office.

"Thank you, Vickram. I'm all right now." He sat down, and Vickram handed him a glass of water. By now, the other doctors had joined them.

They discussed today's incident, and finally decided that they should ask for police security to prevent future attacks in the hospital.

Dr Kimberley picked up the phone and dialled captain Hussain's number. He had to talk to the army chief. The earlier event had left him in a devastated state of mind. His blood was boiling, and his eyes were burning with murderous rage.

Captain Hussain appeared on the scene within a short time of getting the call from Dr Kimberley. As soon as he entered the hospital premises, he felt an eerie sense of melancholia around him. He saw Dr Kimberley sitting on a chair, holding his head between his hands and staring at the floor.

"You called me, Doctor?" He bent down to get the doctor's attention.

Dr Kimberley lifted his head and looked at Captain Hussain. His eyes narrowed with contempt as he pointed at the blood-covered bodies on the beds. "This is what I wanted to show you, Captain Hussain! A bunch of lunatics, the bloodsuckers from the army barracks, just appeared out of nowhere and started shooting these poor victims. They'd already emptied their bullets on these people, and when they found that the ones who hadn't died were being treated in the hospital, they decided to make sure that none of the injured ones lived to see the day."

The captain went over to see the horrific scene, the carnage of dead bodies. He clenched his fists and shut his eyes tightly. "I am utterly disgusted by the savageness of the army, Dr Kimberley! I'm helpless due to Amin's hatred for Acholi and Lango people. All I can say is that from now on, I'm going to have tight security at all the hospitals. I only hope that something like this doesn't happen again, not in this hospital!"

Captain Hussain kept his word, and after that incident, life in and around Gulu became normal. Dr Kimberley and Dr Vickram Patel were often seen together at the weekend. Carol loved to cook exotic dishes for the young doctor. She knew that Vickram was alone in this place and must be missing his family.

Tanya had been away from them since she came back from Kampala. Since Vickram came in their lives, they had started to live life like a family. Carol would often visualise that if she and John had a son, he would be like the young doctor. Vickram had many of John's habits too. He was tall and had dashing looks. His square jawline had traces of brown stubble that he never shaved off completely. His eyes were a greenish-blue shade, and most of the time, he would narrow his gaze while scrutinising the other person. What

Carol liked most about him was his lopsided smile when he was in a happy mood.

As he was an outdoor-loving person, he had developed a dark tan, especially since he had come to Gulu. It was hot in this place compared to the cool climate of Nairobi.

Dr Kimberley's house was only a stone's throw from Tanya's house. It wasn't surprising to see her here more often now. Carol had also noticed that whenever Vickram was coming there, Tanya would sense his presence and would come even before his car entered the gate.

"Hi, Aunt Carol, I have brought fresh *dhokla* for you. I have made a perfect one this time!"

Carol smiled upon receiving the Gujrati snack. She gave her a hug and led her towards where John was already sitting. Tanya greeted John and sat down next to him.

"Uncle John, I want to tell you something." She moved closer to him and whispered in a low voice, "Uncle Deepak has been telling us that there's going to be big trouble. We have to be very alert in the coming days."

"How did your uncle come to know about it?" John folded the newspaper and put it away. He turned towards her and patted her arm. "Don't worry too much about these rumours. Just grapevine gossip, that's all."

"It may be gossip, but the newspapers are full of it!" It was Vickram's voice.

Tanya turned to see him coming towards them. Her eyes lit up. She hadn't seen him for the past two weeks. This house seemed like a meeting place for them.

One Sunday morning, Vickram woke up especially early. He was feeling a bit uneasy. He had had a bad dream the night before and couldn't go back to sleep after that. He had seen a big crowd of elderly people. There were men, women, and children. They were running away screaming from what looked like a big ball of fire. Then the view cleared, and he could see all the houses around him on fire. He saw a little boy clutching a teddy bear tightly against his little body and looking up. Then slowly he said that all is lost!

Vickram was trying to analyse the meaning behind those words. He had always slept soundly, without any dreams that he could remember afterwards. But last night's dream wasn't an ordinary one; it was a clear nightmare! His mind was so confused that he decided to go and see Dr Kimberley.

Carol was clearly surprised to see Vickram so early in the morning. Moreover, it was Sunday! She went to the kitchen and came back a short while later with a steaming cup of tea. "Here, Vickram dear, have this tea. You look as if you haven't slept at all. Is there anything bothering you?"

Vickram took the cup from Carol and thanked her, asking if he could see Dr Kimberley. Carol retreated immediately towards her husband's room, and Vickram sat there drinking tea, his mind full of confusion. He wanted to talk to someone who would be able to put his mind at ease. Who could be better than Dr Kimberley!

It was nearly lunchtime, and Vickram was still there talking to both John and Carol. Both men had been discussing the pros and cons of the current situation in Uganda. They agreed that the dream Vickram had last night had been an indication of some coming calamity. But they hadn't expected that calamity to come so soon.

Because it was Sunday, Carol had prepared a roast dinner. She knew that Vickram loved her cooking and wouldn't miss it for anything in the world. They were about to start eating when John turned towards his wife and said, "Carol, will you switch the radio on? It's time for lunchtime news. Let's hear what fresh plan is being brewed in that tyrant's head. Every day he comes up with a lunatic plan to satisfy his ego."

They were eating in silence. The only noise that could be heard was the knives hitting on the plates. Then suddenly they all stopped eating. The music had stopped, and the newscaster started announcing the current news.

"Good afternoon! This is Radio Uganda and the lunchtime news by Tony Umo. Today's breaking news: President Idi Amin Dada has announced that all Asians are to leave Uganda within ninety days!"

There was more news to follow but this breaking news, had caught everybody's attention. It took a little while for the news to sink in. John sat there holding the fork in his hand while his mind was trying to visualise the impact of what Amin was trying to do.

"Your fear was justified, Vickram!" he finally said. "The dream you had the other night was the indication of coming catastrophe for all Asians living in Uganda."

They sat in silence, thinking about this sudden decision by Amin. John's mind went back to the events of last year, when the papers were splashed with the news about some wealthy Indians. They were taking money out of the country via some pipeline. Amin had come to know about this. Since then, everyone had been sitting on a volcano, waiting for it to erupt at any time.

It took Amin quite a while to punish the culprits. But it was very unfair of him to punish the whole race of Asians. He had been incapable of managing the economic situation of the country. His greed for money had been intense, especially his desire to buy arms from other countries.

Man has always been selfish, especially where money is concerned; then all virtues and values of life just vanish. Man's greedy nature has always been the root cause of his downfall.

With a sigh, John turned towards Vickram, who had been sitting there holding his head between his hands. "Well, young man, what can we do but wait for a while and see whether this news was true or just a hoax to frighten the Indians."

Vickram sat up straight. He wanted to see Tanya, thinking that if she hadn't heard the news, then he would be the one to tell her.

"I think I should get going now, sir. I want to see Tanya on my way home." His mind was in a turmoil, thinking that it was such a sad end to their day. No one had anticipated that Amin would open his big mouth like a volcano, causing an earthquake to shatter everyone's stable lives.

After leaving the Kimberley house, Vickram turned his car towards Deepak's house. There was no car outside the house. They couldn't have gone out together because Tanya's car was missing as well. He decided to go back home and rest.

As soon as his car turned the corner of the high street, he spotted Tanya's car going towards his flat. His heart felt a thrill when he came near his flat and saw Tanya getting out of her car. She looked up at his flat and then started walking towards the side entrance of Aggarwal's office.

He decided to walk quietly and surprise her outside the door of his flat. He stood in the darkness of the stairs, waiting for Tanya to ring the bell. As the bell was ringing, Vickram slowly crept forward and put his arms around her slender waist. Tanya was about to scream, but Vickram quickly put his hand on her mouth to stifle her cry.

"Take it easy, Tanya. It's only me." He turned her face to look properly at her. Two frightened eyes were staring at him. Before she could shower her anger at him, he quickly grabbed hold of her trembling lips with his own. Tanya's eyebrows lifted and then she buried her face in the warm lapels of his coat. He opened the door, holding her with the other arm.

Vickram had decorated this flat in a simple way, with just bare necessities for daily needs. His colleagues had gone to Kampala this weekend. He was glad for Tanya's company. Only a little while ago, he had been feeling restless after coming from Dr Kimberley's house. After hearing that devastating news on the radio, he was pining for somebody to be with him, and who could be better than Tanya? For lately, she seemed to occupy his thoughts a lot. He didn't want to get involved with any girl while he was still on the lookout for his biological father, but somehow Tanya had started to occupy his mind as well as his heart.

He didn't know when he had started getting serious about Tanya. He only knew that he liked having her with him. He loved teasing her and then cuddling her to cheer her up. He knew that she was attracted to him as well, as he had seen that tender look in her eyes whenever she looked up at him. He missed her when she wasn't there, and he waited eagerly for the weekend so he could see her.

He was thinking of telling her the real reason why he was there in the first place. Today seemed to be a heaven-sent opportunity for him to open up his heart. He didn't want to miss the chance today. An idea came to him; he went and dialled Deepak's number.

"Hello, Uncle Deepak! Tanya is here with me. I will drop her afterwards so you can go to bed without waiting for her."

Deepak and Ranjana liked Vickram and trusted him to look after Tanya. Now the evening was Vickram's and Tanya's. He wanted to make this evening a memorable one.

It was getting late. Vickram had just managed to explain about his quest for finding his real father. Tanya had listened to him without any interruption on her part. Her heart had filled with compassion for Vickram's mother. She must have loved the doctor very much to keep it a secret even from her son!

Vickram's arms were holding her tightly. Her heartbeat had increased when he cupped her face in his hands, and looking deep into her eyes, he brought his face nearer and caught her parted lips in a passionate kiss.

They had exchanged a casual kiss now and then, but it had been only for a fleeting moment. She wasn't happy with their casual exchange of a quick kiss or just an occasional hug. What she wanted was for Vickram to confess his feelings for her. She was sure that he also loved her, but something was stopping him from saying it. Now that he had told her what was in his heart, she heaved a big sigh of relief.

She broke the silence that had engulfed them after he finished talking. "Vickram, you shouldn't think too much about it. I mean, the truth will come up one day. It may take some time, but all we can do is to have patience for the time being." She hugged him tightly.

"Actually, in my opinion, this secret of yours couldn't have stopped me from falling in love with you. We've been together for so long, but you've never let me look into your inner soul. You know that you're my whole world. What a sad world for me that the one person I care about so much didn't trust me enough to come out openly with his feelings."

His hold on the slender figure of Tanya became tight, and putting his cheek against her flushed one, he whispered, "I love you, Tanya, with all my heart. I want to make you mine . . . to marry you! But I cannot do so until I find my biological father."

"What will you do when the deadline to leave Uganda comes and you are still looking for your father? I'll have to leave this place with my uncle and aunt!"

"In that case, the best thing for me will be to go back home and tell my dad about you. Once he gives his approval and his blessings, then I won't waste time. I will apply for the visa to enter Britain so that I can come after you."

Tanya couldn't help laughing. "You're funny, Vickram. One minute you say that you won't marry me until your real father is found. On the other hand, you also want to follow me. Make up your mind what you want to do, Dr Vickram Patel!" She took his hands off her and stood, going to pick up her handbag.

"Where do you think you are going, Tanya?" Vickram went over to her and caught her arm.

"Listen, after today's announcement on the radio, I am not going out at this time, and neither will I let you go alone. I am sure your uncle will be happy that you didn't venture out alone in the dark."

Tanya's heart was beating wildly. How could she spend the night with him? But on the other hand, she was feeling excited. She looked at Vickram, who was already watching her very closely.

"Tanya, what I wanted you to understand was that I made a vow that I will not marry anyone until I found my biological father."

"But, Vickram, I'm not bothered about this issue, so why are you so smitten by it?" Tanya was getting a bit upset now.

"It may not bother you, but one of these days, your uncle and aunt may ask about my family background! Then what? Should I tell them that I am an illegitimate son of Anuradha and an unknown doctor?"

"You don't have to say anything. Mr Girish Patel is your father, hence you being a Patel!"

Tanya put her arms around Vickram and gave him an affectionate hug, rubbing her cheek against his hot flushed face.

He was still adamant about sticking to his opinion. He didn't realise that it was going to be a problem for Tanya if her uncle asked her about her relationship with Vickram. She had been hoping that he might ask her uncle for her hand in marriage before they all left this place for good.

He looked at her and realised that she was really worried. He took her face between his hands and looked deep in her eyes.

"No matter how long it takes me to find my real father, my dearest, I am not going to marry anybody except you! So bear with me and pray to God that something may turn up one of these days that could pave the way for me to trace my father."

He sat with Tanya, comforting her, and when he saw that she was nearly half-asleep, he laid her head on the pillow and pulled the sheet over her. He closed the bedroom door after settling her in the bed. He had told her that he had to catch on some pending work and would sleep on the settee. He was amused to notice a naughty smile playing on her lips.

There was so much on his mind that he couldn't go to sleep. When he looked at his watch, he was horrified to notice the time had just flown. It was three o'clock in the morning. He decided to go check on Tanya.

She turned over, and her arm hit Vickram's hand. He was about to pull the cover over her, but feeling her touch, he couldn't stop his hand from stroking her head.

Tanya's eyes opened slightly, and the next minute, she had pulled Vickram down. He couldn't tear himself from her hold. He looked at her beautiful form covered in a flimsy slip she had been wearing under her cotton dress. Her perfectly shaped body was attractive and desirable. How could a normal man control his desire, especially when the beautiful body was within his reach?

When Vickram woke up in the morning, there was no sign of Tanya. He rubbed his tired eyes and was about to get up to see if she was in the bathroom when the phone started ringing. He was surprised to hear Tanya's voice.

"I'm sorry, Vickram, that I left without telling you. When I woke up, I saw you sleeping beside me so comfortably that I didn't have the heart to disturb you. I wanted to come home quietly, before Uncle or Auntie woke up, and I quietly slipped in my bedroom. They will think that I came home very late."

"Trust you to do something like this, Tanya! I may have been sleeping with you last night, but rest assured, I hadn't taken advantage of you. For a moment, I was tempted to do so."

Vickram chuckled before putting the receiver down. He wanted to tell her that he nearly had seduced her, but then his mother's face appeared in front of him. He didn't want to tempt destiny until it was safe and legal to claim Tanya as his own.

He didn't want to get up, but he had to report for duty before nine o'clock. Dr Kimberley would be waiting for him. He also wanted to find out what the newspapers were saying about yesterday's news and Amin's announcement. On his way to the hospital, he picked up a copy of the *Uganda Times* from the newsagent.

• THE SECRET OF ANU •

He went straight to the hospital. There was an emergency waiting for him. He was surprised that Dr Kimberley wasn't around, as the case of acute appendicitis was extremely complicated.

He didn't know that the senior doctor was still at home.

Dr Kimberley had been restless, thinking about the worst. He had phoned the district commissioner's home last night, as well as a number of high-ranking officers. Everyone had only one thing to say: Amin meant business this time!

He was still in bed due to a terrible headache. Carol brought the morning newspaper with a cup of tea to ease his headache.

"Thanks, Carol. I was eagerly waiting to read today's news." He took the paper from her, and putting the tea on the bedside cabinet, his eyes stopped on the front-page headline: Asians Given 90 Days to Leave Uganda. He went on to read the first part of the article:

Ugandan leader Idi Amin "Big Daddy" Dada has set a deadline for the expulsion of most of the country's Asians. General Amin said that all Asians who are not Ugandan Citizens—around 60,000—must leave Uganda within 90 days.

He was still engrossed in reading the paper when the phone rang. Carol came with a message from Vickram.

"You're wanted at the hospital, John! There's an emergency, and there's no other doctor to deal with it."

"But Vickram was supposed to be there by ten o'clock."

"He's been there since nine in the morning, dealing with another emergency regarding a little boy who was beaten by some men of the force. Anyway, I have relayed the message to you; please, dear, try to hurry. It's almost half past ten now."

Dr Kimberley took over the emergency case of acute appendicitis. Afterwards, he went to his office, where Vickram was already waiting for him. They were quiet for some time, each one thinking about the coming trouble.

"I can see the outcome of that dream of yours, Vickram. I think it was an indication of this storm that has come to uproot us, especially the British Asians," John said.

"I know, sir. It's strange that there is always a premonition of coming disaster in the form of a dream or some other strange happenings. One of the patients in the medical ward was telling us this morning that his neighbour, Mr Batra, who owns the car repair garage in Gulu, went abroad with his family only a little while ago. When he came back, he found out that the room where he kept the Granth Sahib, the holy book of the Sikhs, had caught fire, destroying a large part of it. He considered it a bad omen and look what has happened now!" Vickram sounded as if all emotion had drained out of him.

John stood up and headed towards the door. "I think it would be better to take some time off. I had a terrible headache this morning, but due to this emergency operation, I had to get out of bed. Vickram, my dear boy, can you stay behind in case of any emergency case coming to the hospital? I'm feeling feverish, so I think I'd better go home and rest."

Vickram told him to go and not to worry about anything. John saw the newspaper on the table, and seeing it was the local one, he picked it up. After folding it, he turned to look at Vickram, who smiled and nodded his head.

He drove quietly through the main gate of his house, and after parking the car under the porch, he went quietly into the house. He tossed the paper on the table near him and threw his head on the back of the chair. He just stared ahead, seeing nothing. His mind was numb. He couldn't think clearly.

Carol came out to see where he had gone, for it had been quite a while since she'd heard the car drive in and stop under the porch. Seeing her husband sitting on the armchair with one arm resting on his chest and the other one lying on the coffee table, she was puzzled. Then her eyes caught the scattered pages of the newspaper on the table. With a sigh, she gathered the papers and put them in a neat pile. After looking again at her sleeping husband, she went indoors to make a hot cup of tea for him.

Chapter 6

A week had passed since Amin's announcement. People were not sure whether to take Amin's order seriously or not. Life was just going on as before. There was talk of some families taking the train to make a journey by sea. These people had decided to go to India. There was still an uncertainty amongst the majority of the Asian people in the town.

It was a Saturday, two weeks after the news that an army jeep was driving through the streets of Gulu and proceeding along the rest of the streets. When it passed the Singh Construction building, the voice coming from the speaker of the jeep reached the ears of the people inside the premises. Manjit, the daughter-in-law of Dalip Singh was about to serve lunch. When she heard the voice on the Tannoy, she fled the house. Sunny, her five-year-old son, was playing on the terrace. She was praying to God that he hadn't seen the jeep pass by. Quickly she closed the big gate facing the street and ran towards where he was playing. She paused and then grabbed Sunny by the hand. Huffing and breathing fast, she put her mouth near his ear.

"You should not be playing outside in this scorching heat, Sunny. Your sister is having an afternoon nap. You should be doing the same." Upon saying this, she opened the front door of the house and shoved Sunny inside. Then she quickly came outside to see what was happening.

Dalip Singh and his wife, together with the house servants, came running out of the house moments later. Manjit breathed a sigh of relief. Thank God Sunny had not witnessed this horrible scene. She felt sick.

Dalip Singh shook his head. "I hope we leave this place before we have to witness more ugly scenes like this one here." He shut his eyes tightly, but the ghastly scene was still in front of him.

Some of the soldiers had caught a young man and had tied him to the metal frame of the jeep. Another one was stabbing the poor man in the chest, making him bleed. The blood was gushing all over the poor victim's body. He was crying in pain, but the monsters didn't pay any heed to his cries. The voice coming from the Tannoy was asking the people to go to the marketplace at four o'clock and witness his head being chopped off—saying that it was a lesson for the thieves not to steal ever again.

Manjit turned towards her father-in-law. He was still staring ahead at the ugly sight that had gone towards the main street of Gulu. The incident was enough to put a terrible fright in everybody who had witnessed this sight.

There was no guarantee that they would be able to leave this place safely.

"Papa, I think we should start packing now. We had enough time to think about our decision whether to go to India or go to England."

In the evening, they all sat down after supper to talk and make plans for their future. Dalip Singh was still adamant about going to India. He told Bobby that he would feel at home in India. It was all right for the young ones to go to the UK.

There was tension in the air. Most of the people still believed that Amin might change his decision. It was hard to believe that he wanted to get rid of all Asians. Why would he do that? He had been very friendly with the Indians so far! Just because a few of them had been responsible for the present turmoil in the country, it seemed unfair to punish everyone for it.

Some of the papers were splashed with the latest news regarding the expulsion.

Bobby was reading an article in the newspaper, his eyes fixed on the following words:

> Expulsion surprises Britain. The Asians, who are the backbone of the Ugandan economy, have been living in the country for more than a century. But resentment against them has been building up within Uganda's black majority.

> General Amin has called the Asians 'Bloodsuckers' and accused them of milking the economy of its wealth.
>
> Britain was unable to negotiate a compromise with Idi Amin, and eventually about 50,000 Asians were forced to leave Uganda. About 30,000 of them had British Passports.

He looked up and saw his father looking out the window. He had heard Bobby but kept quiet. There was nothing to hold him back now. It was time for action.

Amin had made another speech, saying that the teachers, doctors, and accountants were to stay back. He instructed the Indians to go and register themselves as Ugandans, thus abandoning the foreign citizenship. Many people thought he might not go through with it. They thought it could be very complicated for him.

People were terrified when the army of Bombo barracks was instructed to go to Wobulenzi and attack a family in that trading centre. The soldiers under Lieutenant Juma Ali drove to Wobulenzi and killed the entire family as well as the kids and visitors. That incident made the Asians suddenly wake up and rush towards the airport. They were saying that the man had gone mad, and that it would be dangerous to stay any longer in the troubled place.

The plight of Asians was currently under scrutiny of the rest of the world. America, Canada, and some European countries as well as Australia were prepared to take some of the people who didn't have British passports. There wasn't much response from India regarding these unfortunate people. But most of the elderly Indians still preferred to go to India. They had family members still living in the villages.

The relatives in Kenya were worried. Their close kith and kin were trapped in Uganda, for no one wanted to take a risk crossing the border. There were army checkpoints everywhere. Going to Kampala was not going to cause any major problem. Crossing the border in Tororo by car was a risk at present. Most of the people preferred to travel by train and go to Mombasa, from where they could travel by sea to India.

Thus the exodus of Asians started after a few weeks of Amin's announcement. People were flocking to Kampala to do their last-minute shopping. Within a few days, the shops had become empty. People were left holding bundles of Ugandan currency in their hands but had no goods to buy. They didn't want to leave their hard-earned cash behind for Amin's men to enjoy. The best thing for most people who had lots of cash on hand was to buy gold. At least it would help them with their future needs.

One month had passed. Most of the people had done as much shopping as they could possibly do. It was time to start packing and wait for the flights that were to take them to England.

It was getting dark. Bobby hadn't returned from his trip to Kampala. Dalip Singh wanted to accompany him, but he had refused. "No, Papaji," he said. "You should stay behind to look after the family. What with these brutal soldiers lurking everywhere, it will not be safe to leave Mama and the children alone."

In response to Bobby's plea, Dalip Singh had relented. But he was still worried about him.

He was wondering what was keeping Bobby in Kampala. He had phoned that he would be back before suppertime.

Before this upheaval, Dalip Singh never worried about Bobby's trips to Kampala. Sometimes it used to be nearly midnight when Bobby's car horn could be heard, alerting the houseboy to open the main gate of the house. But now it wasn't safe to travel in the dark.

With these thoughts, he pulled out an armchair and sat down in the veranda. Today he had a second glass of whiskey. Normally he would have a small one just before dinner. With the glass in his hand, slowly sipping the drink, his mind wondered off...

He was seeing himself as a young man in his early twenties. He was the middle of three brothers and had no sisters. His father had come to Nairobi, Kenya, years ago, when the first railway was built in East Africa.

He remembered the struggle during World War II. His wife had given birth to a lovely boy, their firstborn, but alas, when he developed a severe ailment one day, there was no doctor in the vicinity. The war cry alarm would go off anytime, and people had to go into the nearest shelter.

Thinking about that terrible time, his eyes filled with tears. Due to lack of medical care, he had lost his firstborn. Afterwards, the doctor had told him that the baby was too young to fight off the attack of small pox. The chance of survival was next to nil. But Dalip Singh thought otherwise. If a doctor had come in time, his baby could have been saved. He vowed that if he had a son again, he would make sure that he became a doctor.

His wish did come true. Not one but two sons came within three years, and then two girls completed the picture of the complete family. Satya, his wife, came from a wealthy family. It was her support during the crucial time that made it easy to start afresh. She had taken all her savings that her dying father had put in her name.

When Rajvir, his second son, was born, he was filled with joy, and he felt so proud of him when he found out that he was turning into a brilliant student. His wish was fulfilled when Raj was ready to pursue his further studies. He tried with all his might to raise enough cash to send his son to the UK. His dream was becoming a reality. Raj was admitted to Edinburgh University to get his MBBS. In those days, becoming doctors meant that Asians had achieved a high status in society. An engineer or an accountant was considered average, but a doctor . . . !

I wish I had foreseen the outcome of my stupid desires. To boost my ego, I sacrificed the needs of the rest of my family to make sure that Raj got the best financial support in achieving his goal, and what did he do in return?

There was a deep soul-wounding ache within his heart. His darling son had qualified and then specialised in gynaecology in due time. He did come back home but only for a brief spell after graduating with his MBBS. Saying that he wanted to become a specialist as well to achieve a higher goal in life, he went back. This time he did not need any financial support from his family; having worked in one of London's hospitals for a couple of years, he had made some good friends who came to his aid, making it possible for him to achieve his target.

Dalip Singh had not known at first that Raj's help also came from a certain English businessman whose only daughter Raj had married. When he found out, his world crashed right under his nose. What could he do except face up to the harsh reality! There were Bobby and his little daughters to think about. Disheartened, he left Nairobi and came to Uganda to start life afresh, away from all those people and all their questioning looks—in fact, from everyone with whom he had spent his early years.

This little town was a peaceful haven for him and his wife. Bobby had finished his secondary education in Nairobi. He been admitted to Kampala's Makerere University to get a degree in engineering. By the time Bobby came home, Dalip Singh had already started Singh Construction on a small basis. With Bobby's help, the business had prospered.

To think that he had started from scratch and gotten the business going so well made it a shock to hear Amin say that they had to leave Uganda. Why? Oh, why was fate punishing them when they had done no wrong? It was like climbing to the top of a cliff and suddenly having a gust of wind blow and unbalance you so much that you just fall down.

Amin's announcement had indeed given them a merciless push, and they had come to face the reality that they had an uncertain future; some unknown destination was waiting for them. Being British passport holders, he knew his family would be safe, and he hoped the British authorities would at least do something to get them out of Uganda.

He came out of his deep trance when he heard the sudden sound of a car horn. It was Bobby. Thank God he had made it back before it got too dark. With these thoughts, Dalip Singh got up from his chair and moved towards Bobby.

How glad his heartfelt to see Bobby safe and sound. He wasn't the only parent with this tension about the safety of his son, as all parents had their hearts up in their sleeves till their children were safely within the sanctuary of the four walls of their home. The day would pass by but after seven pm, no one ventured outside unless it was an emergency. Amin's men were always patrolling the deserted streets, just looking for their next prey.

"Didn't you go to bed, Papaji?"

"How could I sleep, thinking about you and both girls there in Kampala? Every day we hear bad news about Amin's men stopping people on the way to Kampala or people coming back to their homes after dark. I hope they didn't stop you."

"Of course they stopped me, Papa! It was just routine check-up. I knew they were looking for cash, which I gave them gladly. Money has the power to get away from any tricky situation."

"How were the girls? Did you explain to them why they couldn't come home?"

"I did. Anyway, they are in safe hands over there. As the army men were troubling the college students, especially young girls, the head of the college completely closed it. Kiran and Preety already had left beforehand and had gone to stay with the Grewals."

"Did you meet Mr Grewal?" Dalip Singh looked worried.

"Yes, Papaji. I was there all day after finishing the formalities at the immigration office. Uncle Grewal told me they wouldn't leave Uganda till we leave this town and are safely in Kampala to take our flight to Great Britain. I have left the passports of both girls with him as well as some cash. Mr Grewal gave me his assurance that if he gets the flight tickets before us, then he will take the girls with him."

"It's nice to know that in times like this, we realise who our true friends are. At least Grewal has his elder brother in London so he'll have a home to go to."

"I agree with you, Papaji. This crisis has brought our people close to one another."

The next morning, Dalip Singh got some large wooden crates. He wanted to pack up as much as possible. There were some valuable objects which he wanted to take with him to India. These big boxes would have to be shipped to India by sea.

He was standing outside in the courtyard of his workshop, thinking that while he was getting the important items to pack in the boxes, Bobby could start getting the rest of the stuff from the house so that it would be easy to select what they could take with them.

His privacy was intruded by the sound of a car coming through the gate. He saw Vickram getting out and coming towards him.

"How are you, Vickram? It's nice to see you without your white coat."

"I'm fine, Uncle," Vickram replied, greeting Dalip Singh, who gave him a bear hug. "I never had a chance to sit and have a good chat with Bobby or you. I thought why not come and spend some time with you, as there is very little time left for us to be here."

Dalip Singh finished putting the packed boxes on one side, and turning towards Vickram, he said, "It's a pity that we only realise the importance of time when it's too late. Who would have thought that our time in this place would come to an abrupt end?"

Bobby came out of the house, and seeing Vickram, he came towards him and held out his hand in greeting. Soon both of them were busy talking nineteen to the dozen, until Dalip Singh interrupted them.

"Bobby, can you take Vickram inside the house? I will come and join you as soon as I finish packing this big box."

Vickram wanted to talk to Dalip Singh without any family member overhearing. So Dalip Singh asked Bobby to take Vickram inside the office. He joined both men after finishing the work at hand.

Vickram was curious to know about Dalip Singh's early life since coming to East Africa. It would be interesting to know a bit about the history of this town.

Dalip Singh was quiet for a while. He asked Bobby to make tea for all of them. There was a kettle, and some tea bags were in a jar. There was a tray with some cups and saucers. Everything was arranged neatly on a side cupboard. Manjit used to bring the washed cups every morning, in addition to fresh milk and some biscuits. Dalip Singh always offered a cup of tea to his customers before talking about business.

Vickram was listening attentively to him. He found out that when Dalip Singh came to Gulu in 1953, he had only a few hundred shillings. He was lucky to purchase a piece of land, where he started to build a house for his family. Then one day he got a surprise visit from Rajvir's friend Steven. Dalip Singh had written a letter to his son when he came to Gulu. Steven told him why he was there. He had brought a gift from Raj. Dalip Singh's heart filled with compassion when he saw the large amount of cash his son had sent him. It was enough for him to start his business as well as provide for the family's needs.

Vickram was more curious about the history of some of the doctors who came to Gulu in the fifties. "Uncle, I was wondering whether any doctor came from Kampala in the early days when you came here. For instance, I have been sent by the MO of Mulago Hospital together with some other doctors. You wouldn't know about any doctor who had come from Nairobi to Mulago Hospital and then transferred to Lacor Hospital?"

"I don't know, Vickram. Is there anyone in particular you are looking for?" Dalip Singh asked him. He was thinking about all the doctors who were currently in Gulu. But he couldn't think of anyone who fit the bill.

"My dear boy, if you can give some sort of description of this doctor, maybe we could help you." He looked again at the young doctor. He suspected that he was trying to solve a mystery.

"That's the big problem, Uncle! I don't know his name or what he looked like. I only know that he was an English doctor who left Nairobi to go to Kampala. I have been doing a lot of research on those doctors who were in Nairobi during the forties. Most of the missionary doctors had dispersed to the smaller towns of Kenya, and some had gone to Tanzania and Uganda. This particular doctor went to Kampala sometime in nineteen thirty-nine, just before the war started. Were you in Nairobi, Uncle . . . I mean, during the wartime?"

"Oh, yes, Vickram! I remember that there used to be a curfew in Nairobi. But the actual war didn't affect us in Kenya, even though full preparation was done by the military force. There were big gutters dug by the sides of the roads, for people to take shelter in them if there was any bombing going on. We would hear the sounds of the sirens warning that the enemy was nearby. But the actual bombing was going on in Somalia. The British and Italian were involved. The British Army had captured a great number of Italian prisoners from Somalia. Those prisoners actually built the roads going through the Rift Valley in Kenya, besides the other countless roads, making it easy for the people to travel from Kenya to Uganda."

Dalip Singh was feeling excited by talking about the war. Vickram didn't want to hurt his feelings by interrupting him. He could understand that elderly people sometimes wanted an eager audience to listen to their histories.

"Uncle, if we think deeply, every other community has played a great part in bringing a lot of civilisation and progress to the wilderness in Africa as a whole. All the hard work the Asians put in building the railway as well as the industries around these African countries . . . My blood boils when I think that everything has been taken away from us. Amin didn't even think that our children's future was at stake! What will one family do with just fifty pounds in the pocket to start a new life?"

Dalip Singh had tears in his eyes. He quickly wiped them away before either Vickram or Bobby could see them.

They were quiet for some time. Then Bobby turned towards Vickram. "I am a bit worried about the paintings Manjit has been collecting over the years. Some of them are very dear to her. And what are we going to do about some of the valuable furniture that we had to bend over backwards to buy? The problem is that we cannot take any furniture with us. We are allowed to take luggage weighing not more than two hundred kilograms with us. Without any fixed abode, we can't send any big items by sea cargo either."

"It's not that we can't send big, bulky items by sea to England or India. The major concern is whether the custom department here will let them leave the country. It would be advisable for these paintings to stay here for the time being. When things have cooled down, then Dr Kimberley could arrange for them to be sent to wherever you're staying."

Bobby felt relieved by Vickram's suggestion. "Thanks, Vickram. I'll certainly have a word with Dr Kimberley. Anyway, we are going to see him on Saturday. I already talked with the district commissioner about leaving the workshop and the storage yard with building material intact. We'll hand the keys over only a day before we leave for Kampala."

"One day, God willing, you could come back and reclaim the property from the authorities," Vickram said. "Who knows how long Amin will remain in power . . ."

CHAPTER 7

Tanya had phoned Vickram to ask him to meet her at the Acholi Inn. She was surprised to see quite a few people still hanging around. Normally, it was deserted after six in the evening. Maybe people were lurking around to find out more about the current situation.

Only a while ago, Tanya's heart was saying that maybe Amin had changed his mind. She heaved a deep sigh. *We have to accept the inevitable, that we are leaving this place for good.*

With these thoughts, she pulled out a chair out and sat down. When the waiter came, she waved him away, pointing at the jug of water and a glass that was already placed there.

With arms resting on the table, fingers locked in her clasped hands, she looked out the window. At the far end of the front driveway, a lovely jacaranda tree was standing majestically near the entrance gate. It seemed to be welcoming every car coming towards the premises. Tanya used to look at these trees for long moments, taking pleasure in just enjoying the colour of the blossoms, like drinking nectar from some flowers. She especially loved the jacaranda trees on cloudy days. Their bright purple foliage against the background of dark grey sky was breathtaking. When it was rainy season, the dark grey clouds took the whole sky in their dark grey embrace, making everything look dark and dull, but the jacaranda trees with purple blooms still stood majestically against the dark sky. *I'm going to miss jacarandas if we go to England,* she thought. *I doubt they grow in cold climates.*

The manager, Mr Odinga, had seen Tanya strolling through the lobby. Then he saw her pull a chair from a table placed near one of the windows. Tanya had been a regular customer here. Most of the time, the young doctor accompanied her.

"Your friend Dr Vickram is not with you today?" he said, approaching her.

"I'm waiting for him." Tanya smiled as she looked at the manager.

"I'll order a soft drink for you, Tanya. Just make yourself comfortable."

This place was one luxury that she knew she would miss badly.

"A penny for your thoughts."

Tanya jerked when she heard Vickram's voice. She smiled and said, "Oh, Vickram, you just startled me! I was so engrossed in my thoughts that I forgot where I was." Then she looked at her watch and looking at him with a question in her eyes. "You're late."

Smiling, he bent down to place a kiss on her cheeks. "Sorry for that, but you know us doctors. At the last minute, some urgent case cropped up. I had to deal with it. Anyway, here I am. What's worrying you? You sounded very tense on the phone."

"I don't know, Vickram. I have this deep fear in my heart that I am going to lose you to your family. Uncle told me about the phone call you had from your father. He wants you to go back to Kenya. It's true, isn't it?"

"Don't worry, Tanya! If I go back, I am not going to leave you here. I'll take you with me as well."

"When, Vickram? We've been seeing one another for the last couple of years, and still you haven't approached my uncle even once. He was asking me the other day if you were serious about me. I mean, whether you had any intention of getting married at all."

"Of course I'm going to marry you, Tanya. I am very serious about you. But you know why I have to keep a low profile at the moment."

"I know that, Vickram, but Uncle and Auntie wouldn't know that. At least you should have a decent chat with Uncle and put him out of this worry about us."

"Look, Tanya, tell him that I'm going to come after you once I get my visa to enter Britain."

They sat like this for a long time, talking about the remaining days in Uganda. Vickram could see how upset Tanya looked. He wanted to comfort her, and he pulled her up from her seat a minute later. He held her close for some time and realised that they were getting curious looks from the other customers.

"This is not the place for intimate talking. Let's go to my car. We will talk there." Saying this, Vickram led Tanya towards his car. Once inside the car, she let him take her in his arms, clinging tightly to him. She wanted time to stand still—to forget that there was a world outside this car. She didn't want to know anything else, only that Vickram's arms were around her, holding her so tightly, afraid to loosen the hold, lest their world fall apart as soon as she came out of the shelter of those arms.

What is it about love between two souls that binds them in an invisible bond? It has been like this since time immemorial! There is ecstasy, and there is pain as well—pain in the realisation that their newfound love may not endure . . . that fate may separate them, never to see each other again. Tanya had a deep feeling that this expulsion of her people was going to cause a rift between her and Vickram.

Outside, the lights were coming on. The streetlights were blinking as if trying to tell them that it was getting late. The sun had gone down, tired after a hectic day. It had had enough of the day and felt like catching some sleep as well, making mankind aware that the darkness of night was approaching. It was about time to pack up and retire for the night.

Did they notice the sun's setting? No way. They were lost to the sun, to the world around them. They didn't want to be reminded that every moment has to have a conclusion—that it has to stop somewhere.

The next morning, when Vickram was about to start his car, he saw Mr Aggarwal coming towards him. He switched the engine off and lowered the car window.

"Hello, Mr Aggarwal. Is there a problem? You look in a frenzied mood."

"Sorry to stop you like this, Vickram. If you're not in a hurry, then can you please listen to what I have to say? Only for a few minutes, please."

"Go on, but be quick about it. I have to go see a patient on my way to the hospital. It would have been easier for you to come to the flat earlier on. Anyway, fire away." Vickram told him to get in the car before he began speaking, however. "It's not safe to talk in public. Anyone could hear you."

"I am sorry, Vickram. You know Gulu Drapery? The shop owned by Kokila Shah? Well, her young son has gone missing. Some people were saying that some men from the force took him in their jeep."

"But what can I do, Mr Aggarwal? Actually, I think there is one person who can help. Captain Hussain. Try asking him. I could give you his number."

"I'm terrified of these army generals, Vickram. I think there is one person who can talk to him: his wife, Nargis. I still remember that you used to go out with her ages ago. Everybody in Gulu knew about it."

"That was a long time ago. I used to date her when I was new in the town; she was ready to get me in on all the latest happenings in the social circle in Gulu. Anyway, I doubt whether she remembers me at all."

"Come on! Think again, Vickram. I can easily spill the beans to Tanya that you had an affair with Nargis."

"Are you trying to blackmail me now, Mr Aggarwal? I told you that I used to go out with her now and then; there was nothing serious about it! Anyway, I'll try to do something about it. What's the name of the boy?"

"His first name is Satish. He's only fourteen years old and is the only child of his widowed mother."

Vickram got out of the car and opened the door for Mr Aggarwal to step out. *Tanya is going to kill me!* he was thinking. He knew that men like Aggarwal could be tempted to spill the beans if their request was not fulfilled.

When he turned the car towards the hospital, he remembered that he had to see his patient on the way. It was a relief that he didn't have to go very far, for the village where this patient lived was only one kilometre away from the main road.

He wanted to see Dr Kimberley before his morning round of the wards. In spite of driving swiftly to the hospital, he still missed seeing the senior doctor. He decided to finish his morning rounds at the hospital and then go see Dr Kimberley. He wanted to take the rest of the day off. It was important for him to get the information about Satish as soon as possible.

After talking to Dr Kimberley, Vickram phoned Tanya and asked if she could persuade Nargis to meet her at the Acholi Inn. He then explained this morning's talk with Mr Aggarwal. Tanya told him to go home and wait for her call.

It seemed ages when the telephone finally rang. Tanya told him that there was no problem in asking Nargis to come out to meet her. "I'm going to the Acholi Inn now and hope that Nargis will be able to make it by twelve noon. I'll see you afterwards."

He didn't disclose to her that he would be at the Acholi Inn as well. He looked at his watch. It was nearly half past eleven. He drove straight to the inn and decided to sit in a secluded corner and wait for both girls.

Tanya was the first to appear, and she headed straight for a table at the end of the patio. He was relieved because he was sitting indoors and would be out of sight while still able to see the people sitting outside.

There was quite a stir amongst the people sitting there. He was amused to see Nargis making her entrance as usual. Dressed in dark blue trousers with a sleeveless white silk top, she really made a picture with her brown hair tied with a scarf at the nape of her neck. The dark glasses hid her eyes, and her dark pink lips still had that lusciousness about them which had captivated him at one time.

As he watched the women deep in conversation, his mind wandered far away. He was thinking when he had come across Nargis in the hospital. It was packed with fresh casualties. They were victims of Amin's wrath, mostly from the Acholi tribe. He was attending to an injured little boy when suddenly a young woman came charging towards him. He saw a pair of fiery eyes looking at him with full contempt.

"What sort of a doctor are you? You were supposed to come this morning to see my sick mother! She could easily have a stroke due to high blood pressure!"

What a beauty! This was the first thought that came to his mind. He stood up and tried to calm the hyper girl, and then he slowly asked her about the doctor she was referring to. She replied that some doctor by the name of Gupta was supposed to visit her mother. Their family doctor was on holiday, and he had arranged for a locum to see her mother in his absence. When she rang the surgery this morning, after waiting for an hour, she was told that Dr Gupta had to go to the municipal hospital urgently. She was angry that he had forgotten about his appointment this morning.

Vickram had to explain about the emergency at the hospital, saying that that was why Dr Gupta was unavailable at the surgery.

She looked embarrassed at her folly and apologised, bringing a charming smile to her radiant face. After that incident, somehow they ended up having a drink and a chat at the inn. They always chose to sit indoors instead of out on the patio, where they could have been seen openly.

Their meeting went on for some time, until the day Nargis disappeared from the scene. He found out later that she had married Captain Hussain, a general in Amin's army. It was good to nip the bud in the beginning before it could blossom into a full-fledged affair. There was no future, as Nargis was a Muslim. Besides, if Hussain had his eye on her, he could easily have removed Vickram from his path.

He was amused at himself. *Is this why you have come here discreetly, Vickram?* His inner soul seemed to be mocking him. Whatever the reason, he wasn't sorry for the smashing time he'd had with Nargis. It was a passing phase but enjoyable. It was different with Tanya, who had gotten under his skin. Love for Tanya had developed slowly and was deeply rooted now.

He thought that they were taking too long in their discussion. He was hoping that Nargis hadn't told Tanya about their liaison in the past.

He was startled out of his reverie when he saw Tanya making her way towards him a short time later. He wondered if the waiter had told her that he was sitting indoors.

"Hi, Vickram! You look as if someone has caught you stealing."

He laughed at Tanya's power of observation. He was really expecting some nasty remark from her, but she seemed to be full of humour.

She put her handbag on the table, sat down on the empty chair, and stretched her legs. Throwing her head at the back of the chair, she closed her eyes.

"You haven't told me yet whether Nargis will help." Vickram was getting a bit impatient with her now.

"Oh, I'm sorry, Vickram. I was just thinking about something Nargis told me. Actually, she listened to me carefully and promised to get Satish away from the clutches of those brutes. We only hope that he is still alive."

She was staring ahead without blinking. She wanted to tell him that she knew about his liaison with Nargis, but she decided to keep quiet. If Vickram had wanted to tell her, he would have done so by now. Anyway, it wasn't wise to stir up dead ash. She had a guilt complex herself as well when she looked back at the past.

There had been a farewell party at the college that night. She had finished her finals and was waiting for the results.

Her friends wanted her to join them as well, as it was going to be the last time for them to be together. After that, they'd be going back to their homes.

She was shocked to see everyone dressed in finery. She herself had made sure that she had decent clothes on. But some of the girls had gone over the top; they were dressed very scantily and had overdone their make-up so much that it was difficult to recognise them.

She used to go out with Anil whenever she was free. He was an old friend from her school days. In the early days of her college life, he had been there for company. It was strange that when they used to go to primary school, she never even liked him. But he used to irritate her by following her like a shadow.

It was funny that a person she had never thought twice about suddenly became her saviour in a strange place. It was just a casual friendship as far as she was concerned. She was not aware of his infatuation for her until the night of the party.

As everyone was having a drink, whether soft or strong, Anil had also brought two glasses and handed her one, saying it was only a Coke. She was feeling thirsty and emptied the glass within a minute. Anil took the empty glass from her hand and gave her another one, which she put on the table. Both of them were sitting there quietly sipping their drinks while observing the crowd around them.

"May I have the pleasure of dancing with you, Tanya?"

Tanya giggled. "Yes, sir! I will definitely oblige you." She got up and nearly swooned, but Anil was quick to catch her before she could fall back on her seat.

"Take it easy, Tanya." He sounded concerned. He escorted her to the dance floor. By now, Tanya was feeling high, and she got into the full swing of the dance.

She was aware of Anil's hold getting tighter and tighter on her slender body. It was surprising that she didn't resist him. In fact, she even put both her arms around him when the music stopped. In a flash, Anil brushed her lips with a quick movement, but she still didn't say anything.

All of a sudden, she felt the earth revolving around her. Anil looked at her with concern.

"Are you all right, Tanya? I think the loud music and the stuffy atmosphere are going to your head. I think you should come out in the open for some fresh air."

Tanya was trying hard to keep her eyes open. Wanting to sleep, she nearly slipped from Anil's hold. He quickly grabbed her shoulders to steady her.

"Take it easy, Tanya. I'll help you get out of here." He held her gently while walking through the crowded room.

Tanya was aware of being driven in a car, and then she felt Anil slowly putting her in a bed. She tried to open her eyes but only saw Anil's face next to hers. She tried to push him away, but he held her so tightly that she almost choked. She could feel his deep breath, and then she lost consciousness.

When she opened her eyes, it was morning. She looked around. It was her room all right. There was no one around. She wondered if it was a dream after all. Then sudden realisation hit her! She was scantily dressed under the bedsheets.

Her whole body froze. Anil had planned all this, and he must have put some sort of drug in her drink. But she was sure it was only Coke! She had seen him pour the drink from the bottle straight into an empty glass. The horrible man! He had cheated and made her lose her self-respect. She decided to keep this knowledge within herself. It would have been difficult to make Anil admit his sin. She knew that she had no proof against him. She had prayed hard that she would be all right, and she had a check-up at the hospital before she came back home.

Since that day, she hadn't seen Anil again. His parents had moved to Mbale a few years ago, so there was no chance of her coming across him. She was relieved that an ugly chapter of her life had closed.

Tanya shrugged away from these depressing thoughts and tried to smile at Vickram. "Nargis is a nice girl, but I wonder what she sees in that big ugly man Hussain. He is dark like chocolate; moreover, he's her father's age!"

"Don't forget, Tanya, that Hussain loves her and has given her a life of luxury and status in society. That is what most girls want from life."

"Maybe girls like Nargis do. Count me out. I am not like that at all!"

"Oh, really? If I decide to go work in the wilderness, somewhere in Africa, will you still want to be with me?" The next instant, he felt a sharp pinch on his side. He winced in pain and then burst out laughing. "Sorry for that. In spite of a few hurdles that could delay us getting together, I know we'll always be together. Rest assured, my darling, that one day I will come after you and bring you back with me."

He put his arms around her, giving her a quick kiss before taking her towards his car. He had just remembered that he had to make a phone call to his father in Nairobi. Girish Patel had insisted that Vickram should phone him at least once a week so he could enlighten him about the current situation in Gulu.

Chapter 8

On Saturday, Dr Kimberley's house was filled with all the people he had invited, including some of his old mates: Mr Dalip Singh; Bobby; Mr Batra; and Hassanali and his younger brother, Amir Ali, the owner of the local supermarket of Gulu. There were a number of doctors; some were from Lacor and some from Gulu Municipal Hospital. There were a couple of local doctors who had private surgeries in town.

It seemed quite a big crowd. John knew that this was going to be the last time they'd be together, sharing their past experiences and sharing their problems if they had any.

Mr Batra and Hassanali took seats on the patio. They had drinks in their hands, and after cheering each other, they started talking as if they had met after a long time.

"It's nice of Dr Kimberley to invite us all like this. I mean, most of us have been living in the same town for years, yet we never seem to get free time to make an effort to visit one another!" Mr Batra's voice was full of remorse, as if trying to make amends for the lost time.

Hassanali looked up at the ceiling, thinking for some time before replying to Batra. "I can understand the feeling, Mr Batra. Life was going smoothly for all of us, and we never stopped to think that it could change so quickly. Only when time is slipping from our hands do we realise the importance of every moment we have. Our days are numbered here, so each day will be very precious for us to spend together."

Bobby was moving around amongst the guests, as John had asked him to keep an eye on everyone, to see that all the people were seated comfortably inside the house and outside on the lawn. Bobby was familiar with almost all the guests at the party. He saw Manjit moving towards a group of people, where Tanya was sitting on one side as well.

"Tanya, do you know the lady who's talking to Dr Kimberley? I don't think she's from here."

Tanya looked at Dr Kimberley, and when she saw the woman in question, she smiled.

"I thought you were up on the latest gossip in Gulu! She is Malti, Dr C. Rawal's daughter. She has recently come back after completing her education in India. Oh, by the way, she has gotten her BSC degree in science. What a pity that she will have to wait to see where she can get a job. Now she is stuck with our lot!"

Don't worry, Tanya! I can see you'll have competition if she comes across Vickram." Manjit was enjoying Tanya's face expression. But Tanya wasn't going to keep quiet. She went close to Manjit and whispered in her ear.

"Manjit, Vickram has come across countless beauties in his time, but he is free from any effect they might have on him. So don't try to make me jealous!" She stopped talking suddenly and looked wide-eyed at Vickram, who had come in the room to join Dr Kimberley and the stranger as well.

Manjit watched the changed expression on Tanya's face. She was amused now. Vickram indeed was standing very close to Malti, and her hand was almost touching the sleeve of his coat. Vickram had discarded his usual casual jeans and T-shirt and had changed into cream-coloured linen trousers with a white shirt and matching jacket. The dark brown shirt and cream tie with dark brown stripes enhanced his attractive looks. Any girl would have tried her best to attract his attention.

She decided to move nearer to where this trio was standing. At least she'd be able to hear what they were talking about. She knew it was naughty of her to eavesdrop, but there was a nagging thought within her that this Malti girl was a danger to Tanya.

Malti was wearing a beautiful green silk sari that brought out the beautiful curves of her slender body. She was a typical Indian beauty and was extremely attractive. There was a radiant glow on her face, and her eyes were lined with black liner, giving her a mesmerising look. In fact, all the people present were giving this beauty side looks while engrossed with their own talk amongst their own crowds.

Manjit sighed when she saw Malti's rich black hair styled in a French knot that gave her a look of a regal beauty. She was the centre of attraction in the Kimberley household tonight. For a moment, even she felt that she was envious of this woman. She looked around to see Bobby, and her eyes narrowed when she realised that even he was looking at Malti.

She changed her mind about joining them. Instead, she held out her hand towards Tanya, saying, "Come on, Tanya. I'm going out on the terrace. I've just spotted a familiar face there."

Tanya was about to go up to Vickram, but hearing Manjit calling out to her, she also went out.

"Hello there! If it isn't Veera Dutta. What a surprise to see you here." A young woman dressed in flared white trousers and a black printed chiffon blouse turned to see who was calling her name. For a little while, she stared at Manjit, and then recognition hit her. She got up from her chair and flew over to embrace her.

"I don't believe this! You don't know how I have been asking about you, but nobody seemed to know where you disappeared after finishing your training. My God, Manjit! I had never expected to see you here in this remote town."

It was nice to see two old friends meet after so many years. Tanya was observing them. She was puzzled to see this

• The Secret of Anu •

Veera girl in Gulu, a remote town, as she had put it. She took a chair next to Manjit to listen their interesting tales about their life in Nairobi.

Veera told Manjit that she was in her third year at Makerere University. Two more years and she would have got her fine arts degree. But now she would have to forget that and get ready to leave this place.

"I can't understand, Veera, how you got admission in that university. I remember that when I was doing my teacher training, you told me that you had to sit for an entry examination to gain a place at Makerere University! After that, you gave me good news that you had passed with distinction, but unfortunately, you couldn't get admitted in the university because you were not a citizen of Uganda. That law was implemented after Uganda's independence."

"Too true, Manjit. I had given up all hope of ever fulfilling my desire. I started to attend typing classes to enable me to get some sort of a job to keep myself busy. It was at one of the job interviews that I met my future husband, Dev. He came from Jinja on a business deal with the manager of the company where I was supposed to have an interview."

Manjit cupped her face between her hands, listening attentively to Veera's life history. She loved listening to any romantic tale that resembled hers. She had met Bobby in Nairobi as well.

"I was sitting in the waiting room for my turn when I saw a gentleman coming through the entrance door. As soon as he passed me, something fell, landing at my feet. I could see printed sheets of paper scattered near my chair. The stranger had to bend down to pick them up, but I stopped him and retrieved all the sheets, handing them back to him. I never knew that I had just met my future husband. I think God must have taken pity on me to send Dev in my life. When we married and he came to know about my predicament, he promised me that he'd help me achieve my wish to become a graduate in the fine arts. But alas, my wish is still unfulfilled."

Manjit tried to comfort her. "Don't worry, Veera! Once we are out of here, then God willing, you may be able to complete the course one day."

Veera hugged Manjit. She had always looked up to her dear friend when they were in school together.

She told Manjit that Dev had come to Gulu to help his elderly uncle wind up his small business which he had been running for years. His wife had died a long time ago, and both of his daughters were married and settled abroad. Dev was in a hurry to get back home because the rest of the family was waiting for them to leave the country. But Dr Kimberley phoned with the invitation for this party. Her uncle was one of the oldest friends of the doctor, so they decided to stay for one more day. "I'm glad that we stayed. We were meant to meet up with each other after such a long time."

Carol had been busy all this time, instructing the maids who were helping to serve the guests. Once she knew that everything was in proper hands, she decided to go join the women sitting outside on the patio. She was amused that many of these Indian women preferred to stay away from the men. She smiled when she realised that all of the women had soft drinks or fruit juice in their glasses.

"Come and join us, Mrs Kimberley." One of the women pulled out a chair for Carol. They started to talk rapidly, without giving a chance to poor Carol to have a word in between. She decided to listen to their chatter. Their conversation was mostly in Gujrati and little in English.

Carol didn't mind because inwardly she was feeling guilty that after living in the midst of the Gujrati community, she hadn't made an effort to learn their dialect.

She began looking around at the rest of the people gathered at her house. Her gaze fell upon Manjit coming over towards her.

"Auntie Carol, where were you? Dr Kimberley has been here all the time, but you seemed to have disappeared. I was going to see if Bobby needed my help with looking after the guests. He seems to be managing very well." Manjit dropped herself on the vacant chair near Carol.

"It's good to see everyone gathered here tonight, Manjit. I was watching these women sitting near us. I couldn't understand what they were saying, but some of them were actually sobbing."

"I know why they were crying. See the old woman wearing the blue cotton sari? Her young son was killed in Kampala. He was coming home after closing his shop, and it wasn't even dark. People had been saying that it was the work of the Kondos. They are bandits who rob and loot the Indians whenever they get a chance."

Carol's heart was filled with compassion. She gave another look at the grief-stricken woman. She could understand the loss of this unfortunate woman. She herself had never had a child of her own, yet she was feeling the pain of all the people who had lost all they had held dear to their hearts.

"Aunt Carol, I was so busy talking to someone that I didn't realise that Tanya must have gotten bored and left. You didn't see her leave the party by any chance?"

"Don't worry, Manjit. You go and see if any of the guests need anything. Meanwhile, I'll see where Tanya has gone, if she has gone out at all."

Tanya left Manjit and her friend engrossed in their chit-chat. She looked around and saw that most of the guests had moved out on the lawn. It was getting a bit stuffy indoors, and the breeze was cool due to the sun going down.

She didn't leave the party for some time but decided to go find her aunt. She wanted to inform her before she was missed that she was going out for a walk.

Her mind was troubled. She wanted to be alone and brood over what was bothering her. She couldn't see Vickram anywhere. All of a sudden, he had just disappeared without even telling her where he was going.

Carol had seen her going out and was about to call her back when John called to her. "Carol, can you go in the storeroom? There's a red file tucked somewhere in the old trunk. I want to get some useful contact numbers of some old acquaintances of mine. I think Gillian's number is also in that file."

There was no one near the storeroom, which was at the far end of the outhouse where they used to put up overnight guests. They hadn't had any guest for a long time; therefore, the place looked in a desolate state.

The storeroom lock was almost rusted. She had to use force to turn the key in it. The lid of the trunk squeaked when she lifted it up. There were lots of books and wrapped packets tucked in the middle of the trunk. She took the wrapping off one piece and was surprised to see a glittering silver candleholder still in its glittering shine. She thought that these must have been John's prized possessions, the pride of his house in Nairobi. She remembered John talking about some valuable silver and bronze decorative pieces. The wooden handicrafts were decorating their living room at present. He didn't want to take out the silver and bronze ones. They were gifts from his dear ones, given to him before he left England.

Carol briefly forgot that John was waiting for the red file. She was looking at a pile of old photographs that were lying on top of the red file. She eventually took out the file together with the photographs.

John looked pleased when he saw the file and the photographs. He pulled out one that had turned yellow with time. He looked closely at the face of an elderly man dressed in a safari suit and big boots. His hat looked like a fireman's helmet; he was obviously in a wilderness somewhere in a jungle.

"Ah! This is the only picture of my father. This picture must have been taken when he was in Africa a long time ago. I wish I had one of my grandfather when he was in India sometime before the Indian Mutiny."

As soon as he uttered the word 'India', everyone stopped talking. They came nearer to John, who was quiet for a moment but started to talk again.

"My grandfather left India before the Indian Mutiny in 1857. He forbade my father to go there when he showed interest in travelling as well. He told Father that he could go anywhere but India. According to him, it wasn't safe to go to a troubled place. But Father was adamant about going abroad. He wanted to travel to learn more about tropical diseases. For that, he decided to go to Africa instead.

"One day he came to know that some doctors were going to Africa. They were going to Kenya first and then to Uganda. He came back when I was only a toddler. Eventually, as I grew up and started to take interest in his work, I came to know that during the years he was in Africa, he had to accompany a team of experienced doctors to go to Uganda. A certain type of disease had spread around the country and had claimed countless lives plus caused extensive damage to the banana plantation. The disease was what we call sleeping sickness, caused by the tsetse fly."

"That means, sir, that the Kimberley family has been globetrotting since last century!" one of the guests exclaimed during a pause.

John laughed, continuing his talk. "It seems that an adventure and treating the sick are deeply rooted in our system. Anyway, the cure was found by our doctors."

"What a pity that all the work the Europeans and Indians had been contributing towards the progress of this country will have no significance whatsoever!" concluded the person who had been listening very carefully to John's past history.

John hadn't seen some of the men before. He took his drink over to a group near the window. An old man was sitting on an armchair with his head bowing down, almost touching his chest. One hand was holding the arm of the chair; the other hand was covering his eyes. He was obviously feeling deep grief.

John noticed that the man's wrinkled cheeks were wet. A surge of compassion came over him. He looked at the other men around him. They had to know what was wrong with the man.

"Can I help?" he asked him. "You look very unhappy. Did anyone upset you?"

"I'll tell you, Dr Kimberley." A young man got up and introduced himself as Naveen, elder son of the man who owned the big furniture shop in the town. He put his arm around the old man and looked at John.

"He is Kantilal, my uncle. He had a small grocery shop in Pakwach, which is about twenty-five kilometres from Gulu. Last month, an army force men came there. Their jeep had stopped almost inside the veranda of the shop.

"There were half a dozen of them, looking fiercely around the shop. Obviously, they were looking for alcohol. Uncle didn't have the license to sell strong liquor. Those brutes didn't want to listen to my uncle's explanation. When they couldn't find any liquor in the shop, they got angry and started wrecking the whole place. Then one of them threw a lit cigarette in the shop. All the cans containing oil and paraffin and so forth had been broken; therefore, the cigarette ignited a fire. Within a short space of time, the shop was looking like a fire tornado.

"Uncle had run out of the shop and had taken shelter in his house, which was some distance away from the shop. When I heard about the incident, I promptly went over to Pakwach and brought my uncle over here. Since then, he has been in a state of shock. I brought him here to give him some hope. Seeing others in the same state of financial predicament, he'll be able to come to terms with his situation."

John had listened to this gruesome tale with compassion clearly visible in his eyes. "I am very sorry to hear about Kantilal's loss. Listen to me, Navin. Bring him to the hospital tomorrow. I'll do a thorough check-up of his health as well as give him some medication to perk up his will to have a positive view of life."

• The Secret of Anu •

He was about to go out on the patio to look for Carol when someone called him. He was surprised to see that Mr Batra was about to leave.

"I'm sorry to leave the party so soon, but I wanted to say goodbye to everybody assembled here today." He gestured towards his wife and his wheelchair bound son.

Within a few minutes, everybody came near them. They were curious to know what Mr Batra wanted to say. Carol had come running towards them as well.

"Dr Kimberley, Carol, I am leaving Gulu in the morning. I decided to go to England instead of going to India, where we have our family house in Delhi. Dr Vickram and Bobby advised me that if I take my son Balbir to the UK, then we'll get an opportunity to consult an expert to have a look at my son's disability."

"I'm glad that eventually you came to realise that your son has every chance of getting the best treatment in one of the orthopaedic clinics in England. I am sure that Bobby will help you a lot once you are well settled somewhere in the UK."

Balbir had developed symptoms of polio at an early age. When he should have started to walk, he couldn't even lift his right leg. After a medical check-up, it was confirmed that he indeed had polio.

Mr Batra tried everything in his power to get the best medical consultation for his son's disability. The only solution was for an operation. Things were bleak in those days. He didn't have financial help from any source to pay the enormous sum for the treatment.

When he came to Gulu, his son was already of school age. He could walk but only with the help of crutches. With the passing of time, he grew up to be a very smart boy. Batra's other children had good looks as well, but Balbir outshone them. It was so heartbreaking for the family to see that he could not be normal like the rest of them.

Before Amin's announcement, Mr Batra had planned to take his son to India. He had already made arrangements to admit Balbir in an orthopaedic clinic in Bombay (now Mumbai). His hopes came dashing down because without hard cash, treatment in India was next to nil. What to do now? He was frustrated because he wouldn't be allowed to take more than fifty pounds per passport!

Vickram had come to know about the dilemma Mr Batra was facing. He had taken his car for servicing last week. He suggested that Mr Batra change his plan about going to India and instead accompany his son and the rest of his family to the UK.

John saw that Mr Batra still had a miserable look on his face. He looked with concern at him and asked him if anything else was bothering him.

"It's my middle son, Ranvir. I have just found out that he has been seeing a white girl. Actually, she's a nurse in Kampala, in one of the hospitals there. A Swedish one, I think."

"Is it such a shock that his girlfriend is a white Swedish girl, Mr Batra?" John looked at him in amazement.

"Not at all, Doctor, but he never revealed to us his friendship with the girl. She has gone back now."

"Then why worry?"

"You'll worry when I tell you the truth! She got pregnant, and... and..."

"What is it, Mr Batra?"

"Ranvir's best friend told me that he was a witness at Ranvir's registered marriage to the nurse a few days ago, before she left to go to Sweden. I think she is going to have her baby over there."

"Well, my dear Mr Batra," John said, trying to comfort him. "Ranvir has been living away from the family ever since he opened his own business in Kampala. If he decided to get married, you should be happy for him. At least he's standing on his own feet!"

"You don't understand, Doctor! I do not mind my son choosing his own wife. But I do mind when the son does everything behind our backs and doesn't utter a word. It's not that he has cut his ties with us, but he has always been in constant touch by coming to see us at most weekends. The deep feeling of family bond is still there. He couldn't come and tell me in person about his decision to get married. I had to find out about it from his friend! He knows that we are a very liberal-minded family. I gave the liberty to all my children that whatever they choose to do with their lives, I'll be with them, provided they don't stab me in the back. And if they do that, then I'll disown them from the family name!"

"I agree with you, Mr Batra. This is a total case of betrayal, and it does hurt. But listen to me. You are going to start a new life in the UK now. Just concentrate on your goal of getting your younger son back on his feet . . . and that will be without any crutches! You have your eldest son and your wife to give you ample support. So go with a clear mind, with our best wishes."

There was silence for a long time after the Batra family left the Kimberley house.

CHAPTER 9

Everybody was so busy at the party that no one noticed that Vickram had quietly disappeared from the scene. As it happened, he was called to answer a phone call. The phone was in John's bedroom. He went in there quietly, and closing the door behind him, he picked up the receiver.

"Hello, Vickram! I'm sorry to interrupt you at this time. I can't say anything to Dr Kimberley, as he is the host of today's party. You are the next best person to help me."

Vickram became slightly worried as to why Captain Hussain needed his help. "No problem, sir! Just tell me what can I do."

"Actually, something urgent has crept up. I need you to identify some dead bodies in a house that was supposed to have been empty for weeks. If you come to the end of King's Road, you will find me outside this house."

Vickram quickly made a note of the location of the house, and within a short span of time, his car stopped opposite the army jeep. He was horrified to see that the house belonged to one of his patients, by the name of Giriraj Joshi.

Hussain came quickly to his side and told him that while he was patrolling the streets to see that everything was in order around the town, his eyes had caught a flicker of light in the dark house. He decided to investigate whether anyone was in the house. The outside door was open. The lock was nowhere to be seen. That meant there was somebody within the four walls.

"You know, Vickram, this was one of the big houses in this street that had always been locked securely from outside if nobody was in the house. If there were people inside, then obviously it would be locked from inside. To me, it was a puzzle why the gate wasn't locked at all. With curiosity lurking in my mind, I moved ahead to check whether there was anyone inside. The flickering light was a puzzle . . . but not for long. There was a broken chandelier in the big hall. All the bulbs were smashed except a small one right at the top, which was hanging loose with flickering light."

Vickram followed him into the big hallway while his eyes took in the scene of wreckage around him. Whatever had been left in the house had been smashed: the chairs, cupboards, and so forth. Then his eyes followed Hussain pointing towards the stairs.

He walked over to see what looked like a large pile of clothing stacked at the foot of the stairs. But when he looked closely, his heart almost gave a lurch, and he felt weak and shaky from adrenalin. The light from the torch made the visibility more vivid. He could see a heap of dead bodies lying face downwards, piled on top of each other. He moved the torch closer to identify the faces.

His face flushed with indignation when the recognition hit him. "This is Joshi's family all right, Hussain! All four of them. His wife and two sons . . . his body on top. Oh my God, how could anybody be so cruel to do this?"

"I think that they were about to leave the house and were ambushed by some Kondos. I am sure this is the work of these Kondos who are on a rampage to rid of all the Indians from here. They are the vandals who also rob anyone within their sight. The problem with them is that they are roaming around wearing army uniform, and when caught, we have to throw them in the jail."

He tried to console Vickram and thanked him for identifying the corpses. After seeing Vickram safely off as far as Aggarwal's office, he turned back to complete his task in hand. He could understand why Vickram wanted to go home and not back to the Kimberley household. He himself had to arrange for the dead bodies to be cremated in the morning. He had given his word to Vickram, and like a true gentleman, he abided by it.

At forty-nine years of age, Captain Hussain, the Army General in charge of Acholi District Army Headquarters, had lived in Gulu all his life. Amin didn't know that Hussain's mother had come from the Acholi tribe. His father was a Bugandan and a Muslim as well. It was enough for Amin's satisfaction.

Hussain had proved himself an able soldier beyond anyone's expectation. He was a shrewd man as well. On the surface, he looked hard and cruel, but inside his tough body was a heart of gold. He was clever enough to cover up his good deeds which he did very discreetly.

When Vickram left, the streets were deserted, with not a single soul within sight. Vickram drove straight towards the flat, having an inner fear that at any minute, some madmen of Amin's army would take a potshot at him. It was risky to drive in the middle of the night. Anyway, he was thankful to Hussain for assisting him as far as coming nearer the sight of his flat. All he wanted now was to have a good sleep.

He opened his eyes when the rays of the sun hit him. Last night he had just managed to remove his coat and trousers. After kicking off his shoes, he had dropped on his bed. Sleep had overtaken him.

When he woke up, his half-opened eyes looked at the calendar, and he realised that it was Sunday and not Monday, as he had assumed, and he went back to sleep. But he couldn't keep his eyes shut for long, for there was a lot on his mind. He had to phone his father as well. He knew his father would be home, expecting the regular call from his son. His mind was full of some gruesome thoughts. What would be the reaction of his sister, his brother, his father, and most of all, his aunt Sarla when they find out that he was someone else's blood! It was horrifying even to think about the consequences.

He made up his mind that when he found out about his identity, the only person he'd confide in would be his father, Girish Patel, and no one else. He wouldn't be able to bear the hostility in his sister's eyes and the sheer hatred in Akash's and Aunt Sarla's eyes.

Oh, Vickram, what an awkward situation you have put yourself in!

His whole being was over taken by depressing thoughts. There was guilt within him about why he didn't tell his father about his intention: because he was greatly troubled by his mother's confession that had toppled his life completely. There was only one question haunting him day and night. *Who am I? What is my identity! Who will answer these questions?*

All of a sudden, he started to feel the loneliness of being alone in this place which he had started to think of as his second home. All this time he had spent here, he had never had a moment of feeling isolated. The weekly talk with his father used to put his mind at ease that everything was all right in Nairobi.

Amin's announcement had given him a sudden jolt. All of a sudden, he found himself in a dilemma: On one side was his vow not to commit himself in any relationship until his quest was fulfilled. On the other hand was Tanya! He was bound to lose her if she went to England with her uncle and aunt. It would be unfair to ask her to wait for him. Maybe one day, he'd be able to learn his true identity and follow her.

He remembered what Ba used to say: When you are feeling low in esteem and the world looks gloomy, then close your eyes and just think of someone who is aware of your pain. God the Almighty! Pray sincerely and you'll feel some inner peace taking over you.

A thought came to his mind. *Why not go to the temple? We doctors totally forget that there is someone sitting up there who is a bigger doctor in the world than any other one on this planet.*

He had been to the temple only once since coming to Gulu, when there was a celebration of some kind going on. Today the temple was deserted. He was not surprised, because most of the people had already left.

An elderly man clad in an orange outfit came towards Vickram. "It's nice to see young people coming to the temple. It's a pity that even this temple will become a ruin one day, as no one will be here to look after it."

"I didn't see you, Pandit Ji! I'm glad that you're still here."

"Not for long, though. I will leave Gulu by the end of October, with the rest of my family and relatives." There was sadness in his voice.

Vickram felt compassion for all of these people. He sat down on one side, facing the idol of Lord Krishna. His mind full of questions, he prayed hard to get some answers ... or at least to get rid of the turmoil in his heart.

He sat there for a long time, his eyes closed, and somehow totally lost himself into oblivion. He didn't know what was happening around him. When eventually he opened his eyes, he saw the priest smiling at him.

"The way you were praying, Dr Patel, the Lord will definitely answer your prayer!" the priest said. "I was wondering whether you'll go back to Kenya or stay here. Amin doesn't want the doctors to go out of Uganda. The conniving devil! He knows if all the doctors leave the country, then who will be left behind to treat the sick? The hospitals do not run on the shoulders of a few doctors!"

"You are right, Pandit Ji. Amin cannot do without most of the doctors. I could have stayed back, but I was here for a purpose. Now with all this trauma caused by Amin's order, I will have to forget about it for the time being. My family is waiting for me back home. Anyway, there are other doctors, like Dr Kimberley, who came here from Britain. He should go as well, but being a senior doctor, he will be expected to remain behind. I bet when all the Asians have left, then Dr Kimberley may decide to leave as well. Anyway, I should go now. It's been nice talking to you."

He drove on without realising that his car had turned the corner and had gone towards the high street. He was about to turn back when he spotted Tanya near the confectionary shop.

She seemed to be shouting at someone he couldn't see clearly. He parked the car next to the kerb and got out to see why she was so angry.

Tanya had come out of the house. Her eyes were searching for Vickram, who seemed to have vanished from the midst of the crowd at Dr Kimberley's house.

She couldn't pinpoint the cause of her anxiety, but one thing bothering her was that she had seen her aunt talking to Beena Mausi, the mother of her old schoolmate Anil. What she couldn't understand was that why the woman was here at all. All she knew was that they had left Gulu years ago!

It was very quiet outside. She had been walking without realising that she had reached the outside gate of her own house.

I have left the party without telling Aunt Carol!

Then she shrugged. She wanted to be alone but didn't know why. Her ears caught a sound coming towards her. It was coming nearer, and she realised that it was the sound of laughter. She saw her aunt and Beena Mausi coming towards her house. *To be laughing like that, they must have something hilarious to share between them,* she thought.

She wasn't in a mood to socialise with anyone at that moment, so she quickly hid behind a big hedge that bordered the house from outside view. When she saw that the coast was clear, she started to walk back towards Dr Kimberley's house.

Suddenly, someone grabbed her arm, and before she could scream, someone put a hand over her mouth.

"Hey! It's only me, Tanya!"

Tanya's eyes opened wide in surprise. The man standing in front of her was totally a stranger. The voice was familiar, though.

"You! Anil Joshi! What the hell are you doing here?"

She recognised her old schoolmate. It wasn't surprising to see him because she had seen his mother with her aunt just now.

No wonder she couldn't recognise him straight away. The Anil she used to know from college days was a tall, lanky boy who wore glasses and had unkempt long hair. But the person who was looking at her was a totally changed person. He had put on some weight. His glasses were gone, and his hair was well kept and groomed.

"Trust you to startle me like this, Anil! I say, you do look changed."

Anil grinned at Tanya. There was adoration in his look. He couldn't take his eyes off her face. "Know what, Tanya? I used to feel so unsure of myself when the other students were making a mockery of my looks. They used to treat me like a piece of dirt. You were the only one who never laughed at me. In fact, I used to almost worship the very ground you walked on."

Tanya stopped him. "Anil, stop it! Don't start that again. Not after what you did on the night of the farewell party!"

"I swear, Tanya, that I never wanted to cross that line. But that night, you looked so ravishing and desirable that I couldn't control my feelings anymore. I knew that you would never let me come near you if you had been sober. I had to do what I did that night. I'm sorry for taking advantage of your helplessness that night. At the party, I know we had a drink too much to remain in our senses."

"It was your doing, Anil Joshi! You mixed my soft drink with some drug, possibly a sleeping pill? That's why I wasn't aware of your dirty intentions!"

"I'm sorry for that, Tanya, but you know that I'd fancied you since our school days! I wanted to have your attention for once. So when I kissed you while dancing, you didn't resist. That encouraged me, hence my taking you to your room at the hostel. No one was around at that time, and any chance of being seen was next to nil.

"I know you must have been thinking what I could have done with you in your drunken state! I'll tell you honestly that I did seduce you that night. In your semiconscious state, you wrapped your arms around me. Tell me, Tanya, what man could resist the desire and not take advantage of the moment? But honestly, I felt guilty and tried not to show my face to you after that."

"For that night, Anil, I'll never forgive you . . . ever! By the way, why have you and your mother come here after all these years?"

He was quiet. Tanya was unaware that they had approached her house. She only realised this when they were right at the front door.

• THE SECRET OF ANU •

Tanya found out later from her aunt why Anil and his mother were there. The first reason was that they had come to settle their old house that had been on a lease since they left Gulu. The second reason was for Beena Mausi to ask Ranjana for Tanya's hand in marriage to Anil.

"What utter rubbish, Auntie!" she'd said. "You very well know that I am almost engaged to Vickram. How dare they come barging here just like that? Not after my big quarrel with Anil years ago!"

Tanya had told her aunt that she had quarrelled with Anil and broken all ties with him. The truth was that she had hidden and buried within herself.

The following day, she decided to go see Manjit. There was very little time left, and she hadn't even talked to her friend about their plan to go to the UK or India. She decided to take her car today since it was a long drive to Manjit's place.

On the way, she decided to stop outside the confectionary shop which was in the middle of the shopping parade of the high street. She was about to make her way towards the shop entrance when someone stopped her beforehand.

"We meet again, Tanya. I thought it would be nice to see you once before we go back to Kampala. I also wanted to know whether your aunt told you why we came to your house. I wanted to know your answer, that's all."

"You don't know my answer?"

"No!"

"Then here's my answer to your question!" She slapped him with all her might. For some time, he rubbed his cheek, and then some hidden energy took him over. He grabbed Tanya, pulling her towards him with a brutal force.

Tanya tried to disengage herself from his hold, but his grip was very tight. She felt suffocated.

Anil gritted his teeth, and with a devil's look in his eyes, he muttered, "You will marry me, Tanya, because no one else will marry you if I tell everyone that you slept with me! You'll have no choice but to give your consent for our marriage. Tanya, why can't you see that I love you madly?"

"But I don't love you. It's a one-sided affair. I love Dr Vickram, and he loves me. So get lost, you scoundrel!"

Anil was behaving like a crazy man. He tried to kiss her by force, but snatching her hand from his grip, she pushed his face away from her.

"I tell you, Tanya, he is playing with your emotions. Look, you are going to the UK and so am I, but I've heard that Vickram is going back to Kenya, where he came from."

By now, Tanya was fuming with anger. She pulled her other hand from his grip and gave him a hard push. "I don't even like you, Anil, so stop hassling me!"

Anil's nostrils were flaring. "You have made a wrong choice, Tanya! Dr Vickram is not for you. Look, he has known you for less than two years, while I have known you since you were in your teens. People like Dr Vickram are not to be taken seriously. If he were serious about you, he would have married you by now."

"It's none of your business, you rotten man. Let me go or I'll scream!"

Before she could open her mouth, she felt Anil's hold loosen on her. When she looked up, she saw that Vickram had given Anil a nice punch that sent him rolling over the pavement. She stared at the eyes blazing murderously. His lips were curling with disgust.

"You'd better run for your life, mister! I don't want to see you around here again . . . or else."

By now, a crowd had built up around them. Seeing Dr Vickram there, the crowd dispersed. Anil took to his heels and disappeared in the crowd.

Vickram put his arm around Tanya's trembling body and started walking away from there.

"I was coming from the temple and saw you with that nasty character. It's a good thing I decided to investigate. You should not get into hefty arguments with strangers, Tanya. Your instinct of a lawyer will get you in serious trouble one day."

Tanya didn't reply. She was quiet for a long time, just looking at her folded hands. Her mind was in a turmoil about whether to tell Vickram about Anil or not. But if at some time in the future, Anil succeeded in telling him about the prom night, then what?

"Vickram, can you take me to your flat, please? There's something I want to tell you. It's urgent."

Vickram didn't ask her any questions while she relayed the whole episode of the prom night to him.

"You don't know, Vickram, how guilty I had been feeling. I should have told you all this but never had a chance to say anything about it. I'm sorry. Please forgive me."

He held out his arms, and she went into them, held in a loving embrace. Her head was under his chin, which was rubbing against her silky hair. They stayed like this without realising that it was nearly evening time.

Before taking her home, he looked deep in her eyes. "Whatever has happened in the past does not matter. I'm not a saint either. We do have moments like that sometimes in our lives, but it doesn't mean that you blame yourself for something which was not your fault."

"I love you even more now, Vickram!"

Chapter 10

After dropping Tanya off at home, Vickram decided to go see Dr Kimberley. He wanted to ask him something regarding one of the patients at the hospital. When he arrived at the hospital, he got a message at the reception desk. It was from Dr Kimberley.

"Dr Patel, you have to ring Dr Kimberley on this number. He had to leave in a hurry to attend to some accident victims at the municipal hospital." The receptionist handed him a piece of paper with the phone number. Vickram dialled the number straight away. John answered promptly.

"Vickram, can you come over to the municipal hospital as soon as possible? I have some badly injured patients here. There was a nasty collision between an army truck and a Mercedes car that was coming towards Gulu from Arua. Possibly the victims had been to see the Murchison Falls. Almost all the family members seem to have received multiple injuries."

"I shall be there in fifteen minutes, sir." He sped at full speed to reach the hospital and was there within fifteen minutes. He was lucky, as there were not many cars on the road towards the town.

He was shocked to see several men and women lying on beds in the casualty ward. Dr Kimberley was bending over a young boy who must have been in his early teens. Vickram went over to talk to Dr Kimberley.

"Ah, Vickram, it's good to see you. Dr Shah and Dr Joshi are doing their round of the wards. Dr Karim Khanis the only one giving me a hand in seeing to these injured people."

Vickram put on his white coat and joined his senior to help these accident victims. When he asked about the accident, Dr Kimberley stood up straight. He pointed at the unconscious woman and the others, waving his arm, his anger showing in his words.

"Those soldiers of Amin drive those huge trucks like mad. They do not care who comes in their way or gets crushed under them. It's sheer bad luck that these unfortunate people happened to be driving on the same road this morning!"

It was well past midnight when both doctors finished treating this family. The only person who wasn't seriously hurt was the mother. Only by the will of God was she going to be able to look after her family as soon as they were fit to travel again. They might have to stay another day in the hospital.

• The Secret of Anu •

Vickram looked at the elderly woman trying to sit up in the bed. He went quickly over to help her sit up properly.

"Are you all right, Maaji?" Vickram asked her, his voice full of concern.

"Thank you, yes, but I'm very worried about my daughter-in-law. You must have seen that she is pregnant. I hope nothing has happened to the child." She looked at the still figure lying on the bed next to hers.

Vickram's eyes followed her gaze. He knew the young woman was pregnant. Dr Kimberley had attended to her before anyone else. He took hold of both hands of the older woman, and giving her a gentle pat, he assured her that the senior doctor had already attended to her. She was under sedation due to the injuries she had received.

"Maaji, your daughter-in-law is very lucky that in spite of leg injuries and a deep gash on her forehead, her baby is safe and sound. After a few days' rest, the injuries will start to heal." He was about to move on to the other patients, but she caught his arm.

"Can you ask the English doctor to come over, please? I want to ask him something." She was looking at Dr Kimberley.

He approached them within a short space of time. He was puzzled as to why the woman wanted to see him. He drew a chair near the bed and sat down. Bending towards her, he asked her why she wanted to see him.

"Well, doctor, you may not remember me, but I recognised you straight away when I saw you. It may have been a very long time ago, when you were very young. But you still look the same in spite of your hair going a bit grey and receding a little. I will never forget that fateful night when you operated on my injured husband and saved his life!"

John closed his eyes tightly for some time. He was trying to remember but couldn't think clearly which night she was talking about. There were countless nights when he had attended to emergency cases.

"That night, you had a female doctor with you who had found out about my husband's condition. He was working in his bicycle shop when a couple of gunmen entered the shop from the back door. They fired gunshots directly at my husband, injuring him seriously. He was taken to the nearest clinic, which we found out was a private medical centre. That meant my husband's treatment would cost a lot of money. No one was forthcoming with any help.

A kind person suggested that if my husband was shifted to the government hospital straight away, he could be saved. That is where you, Dr Kimberley, performed the life-saving operation on my husband."

John listened to her, feeling surprised at her fantastic memory! She remembered him after all these years. He was in Nairobi at that time, treating the malaria victims. He looked a little closer at this frail woman. He remembered an attractive woman holding a little boy of about ten years of age. Their eyes were full of unshed tears that had moved him completely. He had vowed with all his might to do his best to save the victim of the gunshot.

Mary had been with him that night. How could he forget that night? The joy of achieving the impossible was beyond description.

"I do remember you well now, Mrs Obroi. Tell me, is the little boy who was with you here as well?"

"Of course he is. We were all together when this accident happened. My husband had already retired. My son had been transferred to Kampala after he was promoted as an overseer with the railways. When we found out that we have very little time left in Uganda, my son suggested that we go see Murchison Falls before leaving for good. My son had this guilt about being in Uganda for the past ten years and never making an effort to go around the country during the holidays. Poor boy must be blaming himself for causing misery to his family. I must talk to him, Doctor."

She was feeling better, so John let her walk slowly towards her son, who was now a grown man rather than a little boy. He was happy that at least the mother would be able to look after her family once they were all discharged from the hospital.

Dr Kimberley explained to the night nurse her duties for the night. There were a couple more nurses on the ward to help her.

His mind was full of thoughts while driving towards home. So much had happened in the last thirty-seven years since leaving his home in England. He could have settled in one place, gotten married, and had half a dozen children. He started to laugh at this thought.

Half a dozen children! My foot, Dr Kimberley. You couldn't have even one!

He was muttering with clenched teeth. As he grew older, he started to miss out on having children of his own around him. When it was time for him to settle down in one place, he was hopping from place to place. He could have settled in Nairobi when he had a firm footing in his profession.

A picture of a serene-looking face was always haunting him. He had married Carol thinking that somehow he would get the memory of Miss Lakhani out of his mind. If she hadn't acted the way she did on that last night of her service, he would have gone on living his life without feeling the guilt of letting her go away. But back then, he wasn't aware of her feelings or of his own. As time passed, he felt a strange emotion in his heart, almost making him want to relive the passion of that one night.

It is strange that we never make an effort to look at what we have within our reach. But once that thing moves away, we want to run after it. Then it is too late, for it has disappeared from the sight.

Sometimes he had looked at Vickram and thought that if he had married when he was in Nairobi, then his children would be nearer Vickram's age. He had missed the chance of fatherhood when he was in his prime youth. Now with Carol, he had to adjust to his present way of life.

He remembered the day he came home with the medical report that would have broken Carol's heart. He had decided to hide it, and he only revealed to her that the problem was with him. After that, they never mentioned anything about having any child of their own.

For Carol, the joy of having Tanya around them was enough to fulfil her desire for a child of her own. She had watched Tanya grow up from a little girl into her teens and then become a fully grown young woman.

When he looked at the young doctor, he'd often wonder why he didn't have a son like him. Sometimes when Vickram came near him, he had an urge to hug him. But he had noticed that there were cold vibes coming from this young doctor, as if perhaps he had some resentment against all older men.

For some reason, they never had a chance to talk about their personal lives. The only thing he knew about Vickram was that he had his father and a sister back at home in Nairobi. There was a younger brother who was studying somewhere in America. It was a mystery why he had come to Uganda in the first place, as his family was in Nairobi. He knew that Vickram had always avoided any mention of his mother. He wondered why, but he knew it was none of his business.

All of a sudden, a depressed emotion came over him. He would be left alone once all his friends and neighbours left this place one by one. He was sure that Vickram wouldn't waste another moment there once Tanya left him. There were hospital doctors and some of the nurses left behind to carry on with their duties at the hospital, but for how long? He was sure that once the deteriorating situation of the economy hit the ordinary people, they would definitely rebel against Amin's regime. It wouldn't be surprising if they started escaping and going into hiding, maybe emerging with Obote's rebel army.

Vickram also left after Dr Kimberley. He was exhausted when he got in the car.

The road was rough and muddy, with little pools of water right in the centre of the road.

It was a dodgy route from the hospital, but people were used to this road now. The town council was doing nothing to improve the deteriorating condition of roads like this one.

It was so different when the British were running the country. This same road was smooth and without any pebbles or debris—no puddles or broken surface. There comes a time when people get used to living conditions which they cannot somehow change. However, they do have the ability and power to change their own homes or workplaces, but they are helpless to do anything about the public places. It was up to the authorities to maintain the roads or just let them rot.

Before he got ready for bed, he went through his contents of his briefcase. He was looking for his diary to check his schedule for the coming week. When he opened the book, a piece of paper fell out and landed at his feet. He bent down to retrieve it and saw that it was a message from his papa.

• THE SECRET OF ANU •

The receptionist had written it and had handed the note to Vickram. That was yesterday.

He quickly went to get the phone and dialled Nairobi. "Hello, Papa. Vickram here. I'm sorry that I didn't phone you straight away."

"Do not apologise, my dear. I know the pressure of the work you doctors have on your shoulders. I just wanted to know how long you are going to be there in Gulu. You can understand my concern about your safety."

"I'm going to catch the first flight the first week of November. So don't worry. Everything is under control here in Gulu . . ." They chatted for a few minutes, and then he said, "Okay, bye for now. Love you, Papa."

He sat engrossed in his thoughts for a long time before sleep started to make his eyes heavy. The last thought in his mind was that he had to take Tanya over to Manjit's house tomorrow morning.

Deepak had taken Tanya's car away to show someone. A young army soldier wanted to buy the car. The soldier looked decent in appearance, and in a way, it was good that the car would be in good hands. He knew that if he pleased this young fellow, then their journey to Kampala would be without any hassle.

"If you like the car, you can have it. Don't worry about paying for it. I'll have the satisfaction of giving it to somebody who can make good use of it."

The young soldier was delighted that he didn't have to pay for the car. But he still felt obliged, and grinning at Deepak, he retorted, "I can't thank you enough, sir, but I would still want to oblige you in any way that is possible within my ability."

Deepak was quiet for some time. Then a thought came to his mind. "Look, young man, being a soldier, I would appreciate it if you could guide us towards Kampala. I mean, assist us at the army checkpoints."

So a pact was made between them, and Deepak handed the car keys and the car papers to the soldier.

Tanya had to rely on help now, so yesterday she had asked Vickram for a lift this morning.

Before going over to Tanya's house, Vickram wanted to see Dr Kimberley. He was relieved to see the car still in the driveway. That meant he was just in time.

Dr Kimberley was trying to adjust the wing mirror when he saw the young doctor coming towards him. He seemed to be in a hurry.

"Good morning, Vickram. Did you want to see me?"

"Yes, sir. I wanted to inform you that I asked Captain Hussain to escort the Obroi family till they arrive safely in Kampala. I thought you might have been worried about their safety."

The senior doctor had gotten out of the car, and taking Vickram by the arm, he led him into the house. "That's very thoughtful of you, Vickram. It has taken my worry about that family off my mind. It's funny how Mrs Obroi could remember that I was the doctor who saved her husband when he was brought in for an emergency operation."

He relayed the whole episode of that fateful night. He was then quiet for a while, his mind still recalling the past.

"I had totally forgotten about the incident because such things are always happening in a doctor's life. I was surprised at the sharp memory of Mrs Obroi! It happened so long ago. I think it was middle of nineteen thirty-seven or somewhere near it. With this revelation, I also remembered a lot more that has been buried with the passing of time. That saying is so true, about being able to close your eyes to reality but not to memories.

"Since Amin's announcement, life seems to have come to a standstill. Everyone is sitting and waiting for the deadline. Meanwhile, their minds are going over the past time they spent here."

Vickram was listening carefully. He was also thinking about an incident that he remembered happening in Nairobi.

"Well, sir, I seem to remember some unfortunate happening during the time the Mau Mau were fully in action. That was in the early fifties. Kenyatta started the terrorist activities and was the leader of the Mau Mau rebel organisation. They had started to rob and kill the Europeans who owned the farming industry in and around Nairobi.

"In early nineteen fifty-four, an announcement was made by these outlaws that all the shops owned by the Indians in the main streets of Nairobi should be closed. They were even leaving letters in the shops that were targeted to be closed.

"I had a good friend by the name of Veerpal Rayat; his father also had a shop in that street. He hadn't received any letter, and he was busy carrying on with work. He was unaware that a bunch of these rebels had sneaked in from the back door of the shop.

"Veerpal's father got shot, and the gunmen ran away. Like Mr Obroi, Mr Rayat was also taken to the nearest medical centre. Unlike Mr Obroi, Mr Rayat had cousins and uncles who were well off financially but were heartless. None of them came forward to help the unfortunate man. What Veerpal told me got my blood boiling. How could the doctor leave a bleeding patient unattended for the whole night?"

John nodded in agreement. "I am not surprised. In my medical career, I have come across lots of doctors who had private clinics just to make money. Only the rich would be able to afford the luxury of those clinics. I'm glad that I was there to help the Obroi family during their crucial time."

"I wish I were old enough at that time. At least, I could have helped my friend in some way! I wish he could have told me in time that they needed cash to pay the doctor. He told me after a very long time that his father could have been saved if some rich person had come forward to help. It was then that I made up my mind to become a doctor when I grew up. I wanted to help poor and needy people."

"This friend of yours, did he finish his studies or did he have to leave school to find a job?"

John had remembered something important, maybe related to this friend of the young doctor.

"How did you know about that, sir? Of course he had to leave school. He was the eldest of four—two brothers and one sister. His widowed mother used to sew baby dresses for a shop to make ends meet. But it wasn't enough to run the house all alone. Therefore, Veerpal had to help his mother."

John mumbled quietly for the words to have the desired effect on the young man. "It's strange, Vickram, that your friend Veerpal happens to be Manjit's brother." He was startled to see Vickram standing up so quickly that his chair fell backwards. He quickly grabbed John's hands.

"That was a shock you gave me, sir!" Vickram retorted, bursting out laughing. John joined in as well. The sound of their laughter was like a cool breeze after a hot and scorching heat.

Carol had come out to see what was happening on the terrace. Both men had gathered themselves by now and were going towards their parked cars.

Vickram picked up Tanya and drove her towards Singh Construction. After parking his car in the driveway, he escorted her to the main door of the house.

"I want to tell Manjit something interesting. I'll wait here in the veranda, and you go ahead, Tanya." Vickram took out a wicker chair and sat down, stretching his legs and resting his head against the back.

Bobby saw him and came in quick strides. Manjit appeared as well, with Tanya at her heels. In a flash, more chairs appeared, and Vickram found himself surrounded. The house servant, Ojera, came with a tray of refreshments. Soon they were talking nineteen to the dozen.

Bobby looked at Vickram and Tanya. His eyes had a question in them. "We are still waiting for you to tell us about your engagement, Vickram. Manjit told us that you would be coming to see us with some good news. Seeing the ring on Tanya's finger, it's obvious that you two are engaged at last."

Poor Vickram! He didn't know what to say. He had come here to see Manjit and wanted to ask her about her brother, Veerpal, and give her a surprise. He gave her a look that said, *Thanks, Manjit, for spilling the beans!* She clasped both of her hands, which meant that she was sorry.

"I came to talk to you, Manjit. I learned about your family from Dr Kimberley. It's strange that I have known you for a long time but never knew anything about your family in Nairobi. You will be surprised to know that Veerpal was my classmate during our school days!"

• THE SECRET OF ANU •

"How did you find out about him, Vickram?" Manjit brought her chair near to him in order to hear clearly what he was telling her. It took some time for Vickram to tell her how Dr Kimberley had come across Mrs Obroi, who had recognised him. The Obroi family had gone through similar anguish after the shooting incident, whereas Dr Kimberley had saved Mr Obroi and Manjit's father lost his life because of the sheer greed of the doctor of the clinic.

"Even though I was very young, I remember when all that had happened. Veerpal is my elder brother, and he looked after us. I feel so wretched at times that he had to sacrifice his ambition to become an engineer when he grew up. Still, he has done very well with his technical skill."

"Is he still in Nairobi? I mean, is he still working as a railway employee? I could go and see him when I go back to Kenya."

"Sorry, Vickram. You cannot see him because he left Nairobi in nineteen sixty-eight. My mother and my younger brothers also accompanied him and settled in the UK."

"That's a shame, Manjit. I would have loved to meet him once again after all these years. Never mind, though. One day we will meet in UK, I hope. You'll be happy now that you are going there as well?"

"I am happy, Vickram. At least there will be someone over there to take us in. We won't feel alienated in a strange place. That's a comfort. But we will stay where Tanya and her folks will be staying. I think that as soon as we land in England, I'll inform my brother about our location.

Then I'll make sure he contacts you to let you know about Tanya."

It was a relief to know that when Tanya went to the UK, he would not have to worry about her. He stayed there for a little longer and then left, saying that he had to go back to the hospital. He was already late for his afternoon appointments.

Manjit took Tanya inside the house. She was concerned for her friend and was glad that she was there to help Vickram get the ring for their engagement. It was such a crucial time that none of the shops had anything left in them. Moreover, the jewellers in Kampala had already closed their shops. The last time Bobby had gone there, he had purchased some jewellery to get rid of hard cash. The ring she gave Vickram to put on Tanya's finger was amongst that jewellery. Bobby had suggested giving the ring to Vickram, who, of course, had bought it from them. Along with several pairs of earrings and bangles, there had been two rings as well. The one Manjit selected wasn't a diamond one, but it was made of solid gold and had a little red stone in the middle.

There was a lot of clutter in Manjit's room. The suitcases were almost packed up. The big trunk was the one which they were trying to fill with necessary clothing, bedding, and so on. There were still things lying around which needed her attention.

Tanya sat down on the bed with crossed legs and observed the bare walls of the room. She sighed, closing her eyes. Then a thought crossed her mind: she was supposed to

• The Secret of Anu •

be helping her friend, not resting. Opening her eyes, she saw that Manjit was pulling some files and books from the mahogany cupboard, which was bare except for some books. She was looking at a big book which actually was an old photo album.

"This looks like your old photo album, Manjit. I'm curious to know how you looked as a little girl," Tanya said, grabbing the album from Manjit's hands.

Both of them were so engrossed in the old photos that they didn't see Sunny slowly creeping behind them. He had come to see his mother, and when he saw that she was not aware of his presence in the room, he tiptoed towards where she was sitting. He put his mouth near her ear and almost shouted, "Mummy, where is my bagpack? Daddy wants all the suitcases and bags in the hallway!"

"This is not the way to talk to your mummy, son! If you look carefully, you'll find it with all the suitcases in the hallway. Tanya is helping me finish packing this trunk, so off you go—and look for your sister as well."

Tanya was flicking through the pages of the album. The old photos were black and white. Manjit helped her identify most of the faded snaps. Some pictures from school days brought nostalgia to her eyes. People and places had drifted away, but the memory lingered on.

Tanya put the album to one side and started to look at the other books and files. There were some framed pictures lying on one side in the trunk. Tanya spotted the top one and reached to pick it up, fixing her gaze on the wedding picture of Manjit and Bobby.

Bobby looked a picture of perfection. His sharp features were dominating the slight stubble on his chin and the small moustache. The best part of his appearance was his black turban, which was tied so neatly on his crown that every folded piece was in place. She smiled, thinking of something Manjit had told her when she had asked her that what had attracted her to Bobby, his looks or his status in society! Manjit had said proudly that it was Bobby's style of tying his turban which made him stand out in a crowd.

As for Manjit, she had looked divine in her wedding attire. She had very little make-up on, but her expression in her big eyes and the slight playful smile at the end of her well-shaped lips added charm to the whole setting of this portrait.

"You and Bobby make a lovely pair, Manjit. What a pity that I never could find free time to come over and look through your albums. Only now I have realised that we never give any importance to those things that we take for granted. It's like sitting comfortably on a thick pile of a rug, enjoying the comfort and softness of it. When suddenly it is pulled from beneath us, we find ourselves sitting on hard and cold ground. Then we realise the importance of the rug.

"Similarly, we had extremely comfortable lives, with our daily needs well provided for us. We didn't have to worry about anything because someone else was doing it all for us! This upheaval has given us a big jolt, Manjit." She closed her eyes, and breathing deeply, she continued talking. "At least you'll have your family to give you support in an unknown place. How am I going to cope all alone in a new environment, Manjit?"

"Look, Tanya . . ." Manjit took her hand in both of hers and squeezed it gently, trying to comfort her. "Do not put too much in that small head of yours! Just have some trust in God that he will guide us and will be with us every step of the way. Think positively and then tomorrow will look bright."

They didn't realise that the afternoon sun was slowly descending towards the west, making them aware that the evening was just outside the door.

"I should get back now, Manjit. You must have a lot to do still—I mean, helping your mother-in-law sort out her packing as well."

"Not really," Manjit said, taking the album from Tanya's hand. "Papaji has everything under control. He even helped pack up Mama's suitcase. It's funny that normally we women take charge of the house and its belongings. But here, it is Papaji who makes the ball roll. I only hope that they get someone to help them when they arrive in the village in India."

They were still talking when they came out of the house. Tanya had already phoned Vickram to pick her up, but there was no sign of his car anywhere near the house.

"Manjit, all of a sudden, it hit me that tomorrow we will be going away for good! A long journey with no return ticket . . . Do you think we'll be able to reach the airport without any mishap on the way?"

Manjit was quiet for some time. The thought had crossed her mind as well, but she had shrugged it off. "Sometimes I've worried, thinking about the coming days before the deadline. I only hope that we'll be able to make it to the airport without any trouble. Bobby was saying last night that we are lucky to have Captain Hussain's assistance in this crucial time. He'll get someone from the force to accompany us, to get us through the army checkpoints and arrive safely at the airport."

"Ah, the army checkpoints. You know, Vickram is so concerned for our safety that he told me to cover my head with a scarf; my face should also be free of any make-up. In fact, I should apply patches of sawdust, mixed with brown flour, on my face and hands. I couldn't stop laughing at his suggestion!"

"Don't be silly, Tanya. That shows how much he cares about you. He can't bear the lecherous looks those army men give to any woman they come across."

Chapter 11

Tanya looked at her watch. It was nearly four o'clock in the afternoon. Manjit noticed her restlessness and decided to keep her friend busy for a little longer, until Vickram showed up.

"Let's go inside and finish the packing. I just remembered that I left the big album and some of my jewellery lying on the bed."

Tanya followed her back into the house. She was looking around as well and realised that the paintings that had been hanging in the hallway and the living room were gone. Manjit told her that Bobby had packed them and left them with Dr Kimberley.

"Manjit, I think we're very fortunate to have people like Dr Kimberley and Carol for our friends and neighbours. It's amazing how the doctor treats all of us like his family!

I wonder if he had a close relationship with some Indian woman."

"Really, Tanya, sometimes your fantasies do take you away from the real world. Let's get on with what we came here to do."

Tanya laughed and handed her the jewellery first. Manjit wrapped it in a handkerchief and tucked it under some bedsheets. Even if the customs officials opened the trunk, they wouldn't be able to find the navy blue hanky. They'd have to empty the whole trunk first. She knew that the check-in point at the departure lounge was more risky. Therefore, their suitcases and hand baggage had nothing except their personal belongings.

Manjit took the album, and before putting it away, she flicked through the pages once again, as if wishing for the past to appear before her eyes once more. There were precious moments locked up between the sheets of the album. Tanya took the album from her hands when she saw the wistful look in Majit's eyes.

"Before you dump this album together with the rest of the stuff in the trunk Manjit, can I flip through it? Suddenly, I realised that I never had a chance to sit and look at all the precious images you captured with your camera."

She began to turn the thick pages, looking closely at some of the pictures. Most of them were black and white. Manjit had received a small camera when she'd turned twelve. Her best friend, a very rich girl, had given it to her for her birthday. It might not have cost much, but it was priceless to Manjit. Being of an artistic nature, she had made good use of it. Anything that was beautiful would be captured with her camera, whether people or beautiful scenery. Manjit was nutty about nature and its beauty.

"It's funny that we have known each other for such a long time and it never occurred to us to sit quietly and look at past memories that are stored in these albums," she told Majjit. "Now that we find out that we have little time left together, the sudden urge to dig up your past life has suddenly taken hold of me. But then, who knew that our days here together were numbered?"

"I agree with you Tanya. We store our memories in these pages and then put them away. We become so involved in our daily lives that there never seems to be enough time. I mean, when we could have just taken some time to sit and think. Seeing these old pictures somehow reminds us to make the most of what life has to offer us. Life could have been a struggle for most of us, but because we had our beloved parents and siblings with us, we were still free of any worry or anxiety that life bestowed on us."

They could have gone on talking more if Sunny hadn't come to intervene. There was someone outside who wanted to see Tanya, and she got up quickly from the bed. Manjit followed.

Both of them were looking for the stranger who, according to Sunny, was waiting outside. After looking around for some time, Manjit was about to go back in, but Tanya decided to go up to the main gate, which was slightly ajar, as the latch had come off. That meant that somebody had been there but didn't wait for them.

She moved forward to put the latch back on the gate. She was about to shut it when she saw someone running towards her.

"Tanya, don't close the gate, please!" It was none other than Kokila Shah, the owner of Gulu Drapers. "I went to see you at your house, but your auntie told me that you were here with Manjit. Without waiting there, I made my way back here. God, I used to walk for kilometres in the past. Today when I was coming back, I felt as if I had climbed a mountain!"

"Come inside, Auntie. It's hot out there. We'll sit in the veranda and talk." Tanya tried to persuade the old woman. Manjit had seen both of them coming towards her and had already taken out the wicker chairs, placing them in the shade of the veranda.

"I'm going to get a cold drink for you first. You look hot and tired, Auntie Kokila!" Before she could say anything, Manjit had disappeared towards the kitchen.

Kokila turned towards Tanya and smilingly expressed her gratitude. "You know very well, Tanya, my dear, how hard my life has been. By saving Nitin, you have saved my life as well."

"Don't say that, Auntie; I didn't do anything. The person you should thank is Mr Aggarwal. He was the one who pleaded with Vickram, and what we did was our duty as well. Tell me something about your early life here in Gulu." Tanya wanted to know what sort of a life an ordinary shopkeeper had been leading until Amin's bombshell.

"Since my husband's death, I had to struggle with the shop and a little baby as well. I could have easily followed my husband, but when I looked at the innocent face of my child, I vowed to live for him. My husband struggled very much working for other people. He wanted to start his own business. After his father died in India, we were told that the old man had left the ancestral home to his firstborn son, my husband. My husband had two stepbrothers who inherited the rest of the property and some cultivated land.

"The house was a problem for them. They called my husband over to settle a deal for it if he wasn't going to stay in India. It was a good opportunity for my husband to start his own business with the money he got from the sale of the house. In fact, the brothers had bought the family house from my husband. It was a relief as well that the house would remain in the family.

"That money helped us to set up this business of Gulu Drapers. We had worked very hard in the beginning to make a name in the clothing market. I used to work in the shop and look after the house as well as my little boy. It was extremely tough for me after my husband died. As they say, when trouble comes, it comes in numbers. But even if God gives us difficulties every step of the way, he also gives us the power of tolerance." She was getting short of breath, and then she suddenly burst into tears.

"All that we maintained with our blood and sweat will be left here, in the hands of these bloodsuckers. What we got after a lifetime of hardships, they'll get for nothing. I wish we hadn't sold that house in India. Where will we go now that we can't stay here?"

Tanya tried to comfort her. Manjit was waiting with a tray of water and some savoury stuff to nibble.

"Don't cry, Auntie. Here, have a drink of water."

It was so distressing to know that the businesses and the houses had been shattered by Amin's announcement.

Tanya watched Kokila finish her drink. The elderly woman then sat back as if it had been a horrendous task talking about the hardships in her life.

Manjit came and sat down next to her. "Why are you worried about where you will live? You are also coming to England with us. You are coming with us, aren't you, Auntie?"

"No, it's not possible!"

"But why it is not possible?"

"Because we don't have British passports, that's why. We're not allowed to stay back as well, but I do not want my son to feel isolated when all the people he has known will leave this place. That's what I regret about selling the house in India. I could have taken my son there. At least he wouldn't have felt out of place over there."

Tanya and Manjit exclaimed in one voice, "Then where will you go?"

"I don't know, but I have something in mind. Actually, my maternal uncle is in Nairobi. I could easily go to him, as he has a tailor's shop in the middle of the city. He is a Kenyan citizen, and he didn't go to England when most of the British passport holders left to go settle in Britain . . . I think sometime in nineteen sixty-eight."

They didn't realise that the afternoon had turned into a cool evening. It was time to go home. Kokila got up and thanked both women for helping her.

"You think this is the last time we'll be seeing Kokila?" Tanya felt choked when the realisation hit her that there were many people she wouldn't be seeing again.

It was getting dark when at last Vickram's car drove through the driveway. He refused to get out of the car because he was in a hurry to see a patient of Dr Varun's.

"But Dr Varun has already left Gulu, Vickram."

"I know that, Manjit. A patient of his is still there, taking care of the place until he also leaves Gulu. Anyway, we will be seeing you off tomorrow before your people leave for Kampala."

As they pulled away, Tanya watched him while he was concentrating on his driving. She was sure he had something on his mind. "You're awfully quiet, Vickram. Is everything okay?"

"Yes, my mind was just somewhere else. You wouldn't believe me if I told you that that idiot Anil is still roaming about!"

"Are you sure? He was supposed to leave Uganda last week!" Tanya was worried.

"I hope you're right, Tanya! But I'm sure the person I saw outside the Acholi Inn looked exactly like him. I could be wrong. It happens sometimes."

"Don't worry, Vickram. In case the man was Anil, he may have some unfinished business regarding the sale of his house. Look, put that thought out of your mind and concentrate on your driving. You nearly missed the turn. By the way, where are you going? This isn't the route towards my house."

"Sorry, Tanya, but I have to see this patient of Dr Varun's first before taking you home. He wants me to check his blood pressure before he leaves this place tomorrow."

Tanya looked around. There were very few people around, and those who were seemed to be engrossed in their own problems.

The car stopped outside Dr Varun's clinic. The man who had phoned Vickram had said that he'd be waiting in the back room of the surgery. Dr Varun had left the keys with him so that before he left Gulu, he could hand them over to the DC.

Vickram knocked on the door. No one came to open it. He turned the handle, and the door opened. But no one seemed to be inside the room. He tried to find the switch to turn the light on, but to no avail. It was too dark to make out exactly what it contained. He nearly tripped over a leg of a chair and had to put out his hand to make sure that it was even a chair at that.

"Tanya, would you mind waiting here in this chair? I'll go back to the car to get my torch. I'm surprised that there's no sign of Mr Ishwar, the person I was supposed to see today."

He turned to go, leaving Tanya sitting in the dark. The street light added a bit of visibility to the interior of the room. It looked empty except for a table in the corner. She heard footsteps coming towards her. There was nobody coming from the front door, but she felt that someone was there. Then she saw a silhouette coming towards her, and the next minute, someone put a hand over her mouth.

Tanya screamed with all her might, but no sound came out of her mouth because someone had closed it with a brutal force. She was frightened that someone from the force had sneaked in and her life was in danger. She closed her eyes tightly as a growling voice reached her ears.

"Don't try to open your mouth, Tanya! It won't take me long to blow your boyfriend's head off."

It was a shock to hear the hateful voice of the one person who was supposed to have disappeared from her life for good! Then she remembered what Vickram had told her some time ago that she hadn't believed. *Vickram was right,* she thought. *This is Anil in a virulent mood.*

Before she could move her head, Anil had tied a handkerchief over her mouth. She tried to free herself from his grip on both of her arms, but he tightened his hold more than before.

Vickram returned with the torch. He had told Tanya to stay in one place, but she wasn't there. He called out a few times, and when there was no response, he grew worried. Flashing the torch all over the place, he proceeded ahead. He was hoping that Tanya hadn't ventured into the darkness and gotten lost.

As soon as he opened the door to the adjoining room, a thunderous voice greeted him. "You'd better stop there, Vickram. I have a gun in my hand, and it's loaded!"

The shock of hearing Anil's voice almost knocked him over, but he controlled himself. There was already a faint light coming from a kerosene lamp which he'd brought to get some light in the dark house.

Vickram's blood boiled when he saw Tanya crawled up on the floor; her mouth and hands were tied. He realised what had happened. The swine! Anil had been in Gulu indeed, and he must have been waiting for a chance like this.

"So it was you, Anil, who phoned me from this surgery?"

"You are clever, Dr Vickram Patel! I knew if I posed as a patient of Dr Varun's, you were bound to respond!" He was snarling, his nostrils flaring with contempt for the doctor.

"I was looking for a chance to revenge my insult of that day, man! I could have gone away from here if you hadn't intervened that day. I wanted to get back at you. I've been planning something like this for days. One day while out shopping for something to eat, I was about to enter Dinu Bhai's confectionary shop when I saw a dozen men of the force talking and drinking beer. Dinu Bhai must have stocked his shop with liquor, knowing that these men were coming at any time and demanding to have beer or whisky.

"I took a chance and slowly crept in, going towards the counter. Dinu Bhai was busy serving one of the men and didn't see me. I moved towards the back of the counter and saw a pile of army uniform jackets thrown over the end of the counter. I knew those jackets belonged to those men. I looked down and saw that one of the jackets had fallen down on the floor.

"I couldn't believe my luck. What I had been looking for days, God threw in my hands just like that. Creeping slowly on my knees, I got out the back door. My heart was thudding, thinking that any minute, someone would see me and shoot me.

"I knew that the kondos were on a rampage of stealing and wrecking the business premises of the departed Asians. They also had the arms to attack and kill some of the Asians they wanted to revenge for some old dispute.

"So here is great Anil, in person, in front of you! Luckily I found this gun in one of the pockets of the jacket." He was rubbing his hand on the gun and looking at Vickram with a narrow gaze.

Vickram wanted to move forward and grab the gun from Anil's grip, but he couldn't take the risk of putting Tanya's life at stake.

"You won't get far, you son of a bitch! The army is patrolling the streets all the time. They could come here at any time."

"Oh yeah? They'll only find your dead body. I'll be gone well before anyone suspects you and Tanya missing!"

He came nearer and put his hand in Vickram's trouser pocket. He took out the bunch of keys, and after taking the car key out of the key holder, he dropped the rest back into the doctor's pocket.

"I'm taking Tanya with me. Do not try to come after me or else." He pulled Tanya up by her arms to make her stand upright. Vickram wanted to leap at him and grab the gun, but he knew the brute would pull the trigger. It was a moment to think rationally and not act stupidly.

Anil put his arm around Tanya, with the other one holding the gun that was pointing towards Vickram.

He hadn't reached the back door yet when all of a sudden, a gunshot rang out through the window of the back room. Vickram had spotted a shadow lurking outside the window.

He could make out a hand with a gun moving about. He felt relieved that help was at hand.

As he had guessed, the rescuer was none other than Captain Hussain, with half a dozen of his men charging into the room after forcing the door open by kicking it. Anil was holding his injured hand. The shot was supposed to knock the gun from his hand, but the bullet had cut through the skin. Still, he was lucky that the shot wasn't fired by one of the soldiers who wouldn't have hesitated to blow his head off. Hussain wanted to interrogate Anil first, before handing him over to the immigration authorities.

Much later, Vickram and Captain Hussain were sitting in Dr Kimberley's house. After giving instructions to his men as to what to do with the culprit, Captain Hussain had followed both of them to the senior doctor's house. Dr Kimberley was listening to Captain Hussain's full report of the episode from his point of view.

"Sir, if you hadn't noticed that both Vickram and Tanya were missing, we wouldn't have been able to save both of them," said the captain. "That madman . . . What's his name? Ah, yes, Anil! He was the one who made the phone call at the hospital." He had figured out what was going on because he was on the lookout for this thief.

Vickram was confused. "I can't understand that. How did you manage to find us without any clue to our whereabouts?"

"Even though Dr Kimberley told me about your absence, I had already told my men to look around. The reason is that one of the army men had reported that his jacket had gone missing. They were having a drink in one of the shops, and as it was very hot, they had taken their jackets off, flinging them on the edge of the counter.

"The shopkeeper was busy serving the men so didn't see the stranger creeping next to him. Nobody noticed that the stranger had quietly disappeared, taking with him one of the jackets. It was only when they were about to leave that one of them shouted that his jacket was missing.

"I was on my usual duty of patrolling the streets after seven p.m. And my men were on the lookout for the thief. Somewhere at the end of the main street, I saw my men coming towards me. It was very quiet around them. The only sound that could be heard was the tapping of the boots in a rhythm. We were passing by Dr Varun's surgery when I noticed Vickram's car parked outside the building.

"I was puzzled and moved cautiously towards the back of the building, avoiding the front door. There was more confusion because there was a flicker of light showing through the back window. I went ahead to find out what was Vickram up to. The window facing the backyard was slightly ajar. With catlike movement, I went near the window and tried to make out the scene behind the glass panels.

"What I saw was enough to knock me off guard. There was someone holding what looked like a woman in one arm and pointing a gun at a man who was kneeling on the floor beside him. With a closer look, I realised that the man was none other than Vickram. That meant the woman must be Tanya. Then I saw that the man holding the gun was wearing the missing jacket.

"The swine! He was holding both of them captive. I saw Tanya slipping out of his hold and just crouched at his feet. I watched the man light a cigarette and snarl at Tanya to keep quiet. He had seen Vickram looking at the window. He must have seen our shadows lurking behind the glass panels of the window.

"Giving instructions to my men, I crept quietly to find the back door, which to our dismay was locked. We dared not break it for fear of the man pulling the trigger. So we decided to go back to the window. The man must have gotten suspicious because he had lifted Tanya up from the floor and started to move towards the adjoining door. Vickram tried to stop him.

When he threatened to shoot Vickram, I decided to give the rogue a fright and pulled the trigger.

"Mr Ishwar, Dr Varun's patient, already left this morning. It was a mystery how Anil got hold of the keys, but the answer turned out to be simple: Mr Ishwar had agreed to let Anil stay with him as he was alone and having a young man around made him feel safe. His mother had left to go back to Kampala. He had told her that some formalities were left to finish with the sale of their house and that he would be there just before their flight date. So when Ishwar left, Anil told him that he'd hand the keys over to the DC. It was simple for Anil to plan it all without a hitch." He concluded by adding that it took him all day to get it all out of Anil, and in the end, he had confessed.

Dr Kimberley had been listening attentively. He threw his arms up in the air, and looking upwards, he said, "Well, I'll never understand how a man, especially one like Anil, would become so daring, knowing very well that with the army patrolling outside, there wouldn't be any chance to escape. Anil took a risk thinking that because most of the men of the force had been responsible for some atrocious killings, nobody would suspect him if he shot Vickram."

They continued talking over cups of tea. It could be the last time they would be sitting together like this.

Tanya was looking around the beautiful house. She had loved every minute that she had spent here with Carol. The patio leading into the back garden had been her favourite spot when she was a little girl. Several of her friends from the town as well as her schoolmates had thought it an honour to be invited by the doctor's wife.

She had come with Vickram, led by Captain Hussain, straight from her ordeal. She was feeling drained of any emotion within her. While the men were all busy talking, she had wandered away, walking into the house.

All of a sudden, a sick feeling took over her entire being. Her heart felt as if someone had pierced it with a knife. She ran towards the veranda, where everyone was sitting and talking. Without looking back, she dashed out of the house before anybody could stop her.

"I'll go after her to see if she is all right." Vickram was about to get up, but Carol stopped him.

"She'll be fine, Vickram. Anyway, she doesn't have to walk far. Her house is right next door. I already informed Deepak and Ranjana about the ordeal. Moreover, Tanya needs to be alone for a little while. I am saying this because as a woman, I can understand what she's going through."

She gave a sideways look in Vickram's direction. Indeed, only she could truly feel the turmoil that Tanya was going through at this moment.

Chapter 12

When John was getting ready for bed that night, he noticed Carol's silence. He tried to say something but closed his half-open mouth. He was feeling tired and wanted her to sleep as well. Before he got in bed, Carol was by his side, holding him tightly; she put her face on his shoulder and slowly muttered, "John, with everybody gone, we'll be left alone! No neighbours and most of our close friends—all gone. And more are about to go. I shall be lonely, John."

John hugged her, and said comfortingly, "You can increase your workload at the hospital so that you will have less time to think about anyone. Look, my dear, even I have a heart, and I will miss them terribly too! I don't honestly know what tomorrow is going to bring for us. Once Vickram goes back to Kenya, then I think we should start thinking about going to England."

"But, John, you know too well that the hospital won't let you go from here. If we make a move now, then the hospital authority will get suspicious. It's better that we wait until the right time."

John already knew this, so he would keep quiet for the time being. But he had a plan in mind to make it possible for him to go to England. He'd wait for Vickram to leave, and immediately afterwards, he would apply for his leave. He was going to tell the MO that his sister wanted to see him and spend Christmastime with her. *What a splendid idea!*

Carol was startled to hear him talking to himself. "Are you okay, dear?"

He stepped over to his wife and lifted her off the ground. He started twirling her, going round and round.

"John, put me down! What's come over you? Stop behaving like a little child!" Carol said, pulling herself from his hold.

"I've gone mad, Carol!" he exclaimed with excitement in his voice.

She listened keenly while he explained to her that the best time to ask for a short leave would be during Christmastime.

They were interrupted by the shrilly tone of the phone. John went to pick it up.

"Sorry to bother you at this time, sir. I forgot to tell you that I won't be able to report for my duty at the hospital tomorrow. I'm going with Tanya and her family to Kampala. I hope it will be all right with you."

John was puzzled. He was told that Dalip Singh and his family were leaving for Kampala first. Tanya and her family would leave at the end of the month. It was only Wednesday tomorrow. He was quiet for some time.

"Are you listening, sir?" Vickram got worried, getting no answer to his request.

"I am listening, Vickram. I was surprised by the change of plans, that's all," he said quietly.

"I'm very sorry about this, sir. Deepak told me about their decision to leave Gulu together with Bobby and his family. Actually, I was worried about Tanya after she left us yesterday. I was shocked as well because even she hadn't said anything to me about it!"

"Well, what can we do now, Vickram? They've made up their minds, so we have to respect their decision. Thanks for letting us know anyway. That will give us time to go over and bid farewell to them. I already said goodbye to the Singh family as well as some of my other close friends."

He put the receiver back with a heavy heart. "Well, my dear, that was Vickram telling me that Deepak decided to leave Gulu with Bobby and Manjit. He wants to be with Tanya, and that's why he rang. I think we should go to bed now. Let's hope tomorrow's sun brings some positive vibes for us."

It felt extremely late when his eyes opened. He checked the time. It was only two o'clock in the morning. His mind was troubled; that's why he couldn't sleep properly. His big worry was about Tanya and Vickram. Instead of putting an engagement ring on her hand, he should have married Tanya in a registrar's office. Then he could have taken her to Kenya. At least Deepak and Ranjana would have been happy to see Tanya secure with Vickram.

Everybody had expected these two to tie the knot for the last six months, when they had been inseparable even for a day. None of the young lads in Gulu would look at Tanya, knowing that she was Vickram's girlfriend. He made up his mind to ask Vickram why he was letting Tanya go to England. He just couldn't see any valid reason for this.

He got up in the morning with a headache. Carol had called him several times, telling him that it was getting late. He had told her that he was going to wake up very early. For the past few days, he had been missing his morning walk. He must resume his daily routine.

"You can't go for a walk, John, because we are already late. Remember, we have to see Tanya before you go to the hospital."

"Sorry, Carol. I'll get changed quickly and join you at the breakfast table within half an hour."

Carol smiled. She knew he would be ready within ten minutes. Punctuality was one of his best virtues. Doctors did not have any spare time to think about personal appearance. Duty came first. She was proud of her husband, who was a doctor first and then her husband!

It was a terribly emotional scene at Deepak's house. The packed luggage was assembled outside in the porch. The living room, where there was all the necessary furniture, was almost bare except a few old chairs. The kitchen was untouched. It was left fully equipped, with kitchen utensils and crockery in the cupboards. Most of the people had left their kitchens like this. They had managed to give away the furniture to their house servants or anyone in need of such items.

Vickram was standing outside in the front garden, talking to Dr Kimberley. The older man said, "I've just been to see Bobby and Manjit. They were all standing outside their house, waiting for the taxi. I happened to see Bobby's father cuddling Prince. His eyes were full of pain, and tears were falling on the dog's coat. Sunny was crying, asking why Prince couldn't come with them. Manjit took him to one side to comfort him. I'm not a very emotional person myself, but that scene moved me so much that my throat choked. That dog has been a most lovable pet, not only for the family but for our lot as well."

Vickram almost said to Dr Kimberley that he couldn't see the pain of losing a pet animal. How would he cope with his own emotions when he had to say goodbye to Tanya? But he kept quiet. His heart almost wept when he saw Tanya in Carol's arms. She was sobbing, her heart clearly breaking. His heart was getting heavy when finally they all sat in the waiting car.

Vickram was going to follow them. Tanya had refused to sit with him, saying that they were not a married couple. It was a sharp retort. Vickram must have felt the impact of those words. He knew that Tanya had every right to be angry with him. He knew the reason for her offensive behaviour but couldn't do anything.

He had noticed the remorseful looks that Deepak and Tanya were giving him. He was feeling wretched within himself for giving them this grief. He had tried his best to explain to Deepak that without his father's consent, he couldn't marry Tanya. He already had declared his love for her and had sealed the relationship by putting a ring on her finger. He couldn't do any more than that except give them the assurance of following them as soon as he got his visa to enter Britain.

Deepak shook hands with John, saying, "I am very sorry that we had to change our plan at the last moment. There was a lot of cash still left even after finishing all the formalities. Then Ranjana came up with this idea that we should spend the remaining cash to do some shopping in Kampala. At least we could have some personal clothing to fulfil our requirements in the cold weather of England. Tanya welcomed the chance to do more shopping because she couldn't get much in Gulu. We thought it was better to be together—I mean, Bobby's family and us, staying together in Kampala. We still have a couple of days before getting on the plane."

"It's all right, Deepak. You don't have to feel guilty about it. I can understand why you had to make a quick decision. It's only that I was thinking that we wouldn't even get a chance to say our goodbyes."

Vickram was behind all of them. Bobby was driving ahead of the taxi, transporting their luggage and his parents. There wasn't much room in the taxi, so the children had to go with their mum and dad.

There was someone following them in an army jeep. Deepak had told him about his car which he had given to one of the men from the force. He was supposed to see them through the checkpoints and as far as Kampala. It was a relief that they'd have security today. When they got to the airport, Captain Hussain was going to meet them there. He had phoned Vickram and said that Nargis would accompany him, as she wanted to say goodbye to Tanya and Manjit.

He was still cautious of the passing army trucks and jeeps. There was always fear lurking around while they were still in Uganda.

When eventually they arrived in Kampala, it was almost evening. It was thoughtful of Mr Grewal to leave the keys with a neighbour who had worked in his car showroom. Bobby went over to get the keys and let everyone in.

"Are there any beds in the rooms, Bobby?" Dalip Singh had walked ahead, and he was feeling tired. He looked around and was surprised to see that there was a lot of furniture still around.

Bobby went over to his father and helped him sit down. His mother and Ranjana went to find the kitchen. They were thrilled to find that the kitchen had everything for their stay until Sunday, when they'd go to Entebbe airport.

They were all having dinner together. Dalip Singh's heart was full of gratitude towards Mr Grewal and the way he had left everything as if they were still living there. He knew that Grewal was rich and had a big heart as well. He was still confused about this house, however. Bobby put his mind at rest by telling him that Mr Grewal had given the house to one of the doctors at Mulago Hospital. The doctor had come from Kenya, and over the past several years, he had become very close to the Grewal family.

Looking at them, Vickram felt a pang in his heart. Lately he had started to miss his father very much. He was getting restless and a bit irritated as well. Maybe his annoyance had more to do with Tanya's aloofness. Before she left, he must talk to her.

He decided to go see Deepak and ask him if he could talk to Tanya in private. The pleading look in his eyes was enough for Deepak to give his consent.

The room which Vickram was given was one of the smaller ones adjoining the master bedroom. There were four more rooms besides the one which Vickram had. He didn't see Tanya coming into the room, as his back was towards her. He had been looking out the window at the beautiful houses all around this hilly area of Kampala.

"You wanted to see me, Vickram?" Tanya's voice sounded so sad that he shut his eyes tightly. There was anger burning within him. He wanted to ask her the reason for her aloofness.

He turned to see her standing near the door. Without saying anything, he went towards the door to close it before pulling her roughly in his arms.

"You're hurting me, Vickram!"

Before she could say anything else, he closed his mouth around hers. The pent-up emotions of so many days had finally broken his reserve. After a little while, his hold became loose. He made her sit on the bed and took her hands in his.

"I do understand your uncle and aunt's concern for your future," he said. "I am going to ask you one thing now, Tanya. Tell me, do you really love me . . . and trust me as well?"

"Of course I do, Vickram. How could you ask me that?"

"I'm asking you that because if you really love me, then you will have trust in me as well. If you have trust in my love for you, then you should never doubt me. I told you that the minute I get my visa to enter Britain, I am coming straight over to get you. No matter where you will be staying, I shall find you. It is up to you whether you believe me or not."

All of a sudden, Tanya threw her head on his shoulder. "I am so sorry, Vickram, that I doubted you! It's the way uncle and auntie asked me all those questions that were difficult to answer. That's why I became unsure of myself, of my ability to wait for you in a strange place."

They stayed like that, engrossed in each other, forgetting that there was a world out there. Nothing existed for these two. They wanted time to stand still so they could savour this moment until eternity. But alas, they had to come back to the reality of the present time. Vickram wanted to spend every minute with Tanya before they had to be at the airport.

Bobby had gone outside to see if the taxi had arrived for his parents. Their flight to India was in the evening. They had to be at the airport by four in the afternoon. He had asked Vickram and Tanya to keep an eye on the children in their absence.

These three days Vickram spent with all of them were memorable for him. He wasn't new to Kampala, having stayed there for nearly eighteen months, but wherever Tanya took him now was new to him. He never knew that going to see an Indian movie could be that much fun.

They were sitting on the open ground in a small park opposite a big cinema hall. There was a small fish and chips shop on the left side of the main door of the cinema.

"On Sundays, we always came here to spend the evening with our friends. It's amazing that a crowd would build in the early afternoon, waiting for the cinema doors to open. Those people who couldn't get the tickets would sit back here, on these benches, and wait for the next show. The fish and chips shop would get jam-packed! Ah, that lovely aroma of hot chips with tomato sauce and vinegar was yummy..."

Tanya had thrown her head backwards, and with her eyes closed, she seemed to be savouring those past moments. There was a smell of chips near her. She opened her eyes and was startled to see two greyish-blue eyes looking into hers.

"A surprise treat for you, madam." Vickram was standing in front of her. He handed her something wrapped in a newspaper.

Tanya thanked Vickram, taking the wrapped package from him. Her eyes were moist when she opened it and saw fresh hot chips with vinegar and tomato sauce.

"Bobby, learn something from Vickram!" Manjit remarked, looking at her husband.

They had a lovely time shopping in a big department store. The smaller shops were all gone; the Indian owners had sold off their goods, and in some cases, the vandals had smashed the shop windows and gotten away with expensive stuff that was mostly electrical. The big stores were the only ones that were operating until the deadline commenced on 9 November.

"We never had enough time to come to Kampala to do any decent shopping," Manjit said while browsing through the women and children's section. Apart from Manjit and

Tanya, nobody wanted anything, as their baggage was already the maximum weight allowed by the airlines.

They were disappointed that they didn't have much warm clothing with them. Still, the cardigans and jumpers should be enough to help them face the cold climate of England.

It was late at night. The children had gone to sleep, but the rest of them were having coffee in the drawing room. Sleep was the last thing they had in mind. They were exchanging so many tales that it was as if they had just met.

Vickram was listening to some gregarious tales which Deepak was telling them. It was amazing that in the day-to-day life of an individual, one never has time to sit and have a frank conversation. He was regretting this now, wishing that he had made the extra effort to get to know all these people. Apart from Tanya, how much did he know about anyone else in Gulu!

Somewhere in his mind, he defended himself, rationalising that he had come to Uganda with a purpose. His mind had refused to acknowledge that there was life out there for him to enjoy if only he allowed himself. And tomorrow everyone would be busy getting ready and checking their bags for the one-way journey to the UK.

Deepak was watching Vickram. All of a sudden, he had realised that he didn't know Vickram very well. "I know it's a bit late for me to be asking you this, Vickram, but you never talk about your family. All this time we've known you, the only information about you is that your father is in Nairobi. You've never talked about your mother or your siblings ... if you have any at all?"

Tanya looked at her uncle. She wanted to stop him from asking Vickram anything, but it was too late. He had already told Tanya about his family, and he wasn't in a mood to talk about it anymore.

"I have told Tanya all about my family, so she should be the one you'd ask." He got up and went straight to his room.

Tanya explained to her uncle that Vickram easily got emotional about his mother, saying it was her fault for not telling both of them about Vickram's family.

"I've been telling you, Tanya, that there is some mystery surrounding that man. First of all, he has a secure family in Nairobi and a good job in a hospital as well. Then why on earth did he have to leave everything behind to come to Uganda?"

"Please, Uncle," Tanya pleaded with him, "don't say anything now, I beg of you! I will tell you everything one of these days. Just trust me. I know Vickram very well and have complete trust in him."

She was feeling really tired now, and Manjit and Bobby got up to go to bed as well. Deepak was the last person to go to his room.

What a sad end to a cheerful evening. Ranjana was annoyed with her husband. She knew he had upset Vickram. But she also knew that he was worried about his niece as well.

It was okay for Vickram to say that he would come after them and marry Tanya with their blessing. But who knew whether he'd get a visa or not? There were always loopholes in these matters, especially with the current law in Kenya.

Chapter 13

There was a lot of commotion at the end of the queue, with passengers getting impatient to get their luggage checked quickly. Somehow, in these circumstances, every normal person seems to lose patience. They all know very well that the plane will not leave them behind.

Tanya was standing behind her uncle while Vickram tried to clear the way for everyone to move forward at a steady pace. He was surprised to see many familiar faces amongst the people there.

Tanya was feeling sick, with a nauseating feeling overtaking her. She sat down at the end of the luggage trolley. When Vickram saw her, he quickly came to help and walked her towards one of the chairs in the waiting lounge.

Bobby and Manjit were way ahead of them. Manjit was engrossed with her children, and Bobby decided to walk away a little to see why they were still standing in one position.

There were only a handful of officers dealing with the passengers at the baggage checkpoint. He saw that there were two men preventing the queue from moving forward. There must be some passport problem. He shrugged the thought from his mind and turned to greet someone he had recognised. He became so involved in the conversation with this person that he didn't see half a dozen fierce-looking commandos marching towards the immigration officer.

It seemed someone had reported the problem to the army. Within a moment, a shower of bullets was coming towards those two unfortunate men. Within a short space of time, their bodies fell on the ground in a heap. It all looked like a slow motion picture.

The atmosphere was like calmness after a storm. The effect of the gunshots was so devastating that people standing there felt their heartbeats had stopped. They were holding their collective breath, dreading another thundering sound coming from the guns. The frightened passengers had their eyes tightly shut, expecting that any minute the bullets would tear their bodies to shreds.

It was only a minute or so before there was commotion where the bodies had fallen. Bobby saw those soldiers marching out of the lounge. They were looking with animosity towards the rest of the people in the lounge.

Vickram spotted Captain Hussain standing near the entrance of the lounge. He waved his hands, and within a minute, Hussain was rushing towards him, Nargis in tow.

"I'm so sorry, Vickram, for what had happened just now. I confronted those soldiers as they were getting in their jeep, for the sound of the gunshots could be heard from far away. They said that they had been on the lookout for these two men. For several days, they had been on the run after the soldiers warned them that all the gold in their shops should be surrendered before leaving the country.

"To any onlooker, it would have been a normal scene at the shop, with the shutters down and the large windows showing all the jewellery displayed neatly in rows. Then one day, the shutters were down. The soldiers knew that the owners had packed up and gone. They decided to look inside the shop. It was easy to break the lock using a pistol. One shot, and the lock fell. They got a shock when they saw the inside of the shop. It was bare of any valuables.

"Everybody knows that each person is supposed to take only fifty pounds in cash money in the pocket when leaving the country. As for the baggage, it is thoroughly checked, and if there is any hidden money or gold, it will be seized. These two men had hidden that gold in their trunk that was opened on suspicion after the custom officer received an anonymous call."

"I can understand the fury of the army men, but to shoot them like this when they were going to leave the country! Anyway, what's more, the gold had been seized, so shouldn't that be enough? It is so easy to grab what's not yours, but for those people who spent their entire lives working to earn a living, just think how difficult it could have been for them to leave everything behind."

Hussain was quiet for some time. He knew that what Vickram was saying was true, but the savage men of Amin's brutal army were beyond any humane consideration towards the Asians just now. They needed only a little excuse to open fire on anyone who was in their way. The firearms were like toys to them.

"This is why I am anxious for all of you people to leave this country as soon as possible. I have an Indian wife, and I can understand the agony she must be feeling as well. I wish I had come a bit earlier. I could have stopped those men from coming near the immigration counter. There are already officers appointed here."

Vickram was feeling uneasy and wanted the formalities to finish soon. By that time, the people started to move more rapidly towards the immigration checkpoint, and he called to Tanya to come and join her uncle and aunt.

He wasn't allowed to go beyond the immigration checkpoint as everyone moved towards the departure gate. They passed him one by one, and when Bobby and Manjit approached him, he gave a bear hug to Bobby and whispered in his ear.

"My dear Bobby, I am sending Tanya alone because I know you'll be there to look after her. Her uncle and aunt are with her, but I know she will feel lonely in a strange place. I'm going to miss her very much but only until Christmastime.

Do send me your contact number as soon as you land in England. You will do this much for me, Bobby?"

There was a lump in Bobby's throat. Taking Vickram by both of his shoulders, he looked deep in his eyes.

"Of course I will look after Tanya, Bobby! She has always been like a sister to me, like Kiran and Preety. So put that worry out of your mind, go back to Kenya, and prepare to come after Tanya as soon as possible."

Leaving him at the barrier point, Bobby moved on. He knew Tanya was waiting to say her farewell to Vickram, so he moved quickly to follow his wife and his children. He didn't want to witness another emotional scene. He shouldn't have worried because Tanya just faced Vickram without saying anything. So much in her heart was dying to get out of her system, and she was afraid that in doing so, she could miss her flight. Her look told Vickram all she wanted to say to him. After a heart-piercing look, she was on her way towards the passport immigration.

He stood there for a long time, until the last of the passengers had disappeared behind the door. His mind had gone numb for the time being. He was asking himself whether he had done the right thing in letting Tanya go to England. It would have been easy to take her back home to Kenya, where he could have married her with his father's blessing.

He went back in the lounge, and finding an empty place, he sat down. He was feeling so tired in mind and body. Tanya's face was haunting him. Her eyes had looked blankly at him, and then a pained expression came over her face, making his heart fill with remorse. He wished there were a way out of his dilemma. However, before he could think of marriage with a clear conscience, his first priority was to find his biological father.

"Oh, damn it!" He banged his fist on the wooden armrest of the chair he was sitting on.

"Are you all right, son?"

He was feeling embarrassed when he realised that he had spoken aloud. He looked at the elderly man who was watching him closely, and before he could explain his outburst, the stranger spoke again.

"Pardon my impertinence, young man, but for a moment, I was taken aback. You have a terrific resemblance to someone I used to know years ago."

Vickram felt as if he had woken up from a deep sleep. He sat up straight and cleared his throat. Thousands of questions had suddenly taken over his thinking power. "I'm sorry for my funny behaviour, sir, but did you say you knew someone who looked like me? Please tell me more!"

The stranger put out his hand towards Vickram and said, "I'm Dr Mehta. I came to see off my brother and his family. He's a lawyer and has been running his business in Jinja for the last twenty years. Just like everybody else, he also had to wind up his business and join the exodus of British Asians—"

"Sorry to interrupt you, sir, but have you been in Uganda for long?"

"No, I came from Nairobi to meet my brother before Amin made that announcement. We thought that there would be very little time left for us to be together. Only God knows when we will be together again, so my brother insisted that I extend my stay until the last day so I could say my final farewell while seeing them off at the airport."

The elderly doctor paused for a while. Maybe he was feeling the pain of separation from his loved ones. Looking around him, he quickly took a handkerchief from his trouser pocket and blew his nose.

"I am sorry. All of a sudden, I had this dreadful feeling as if someone had snatched my heart from my body. A feeling of emptiness suddenly took over my entire being. Anyway, that's life. We are bound to be separated from our loved ones sooner or later. Only destiny knows if we'll ever meet again."

Vickram agreed with the doctor. "The feeling is mutual, sir. But I was puzzled when you said that I looked like someone you knew. Can you explain this? I'm sorry for my persistent attitude. I'll explain the reason later, but please tell me about this person you mentioned a while ago." Vickram's heart rate had increased. He had a gut feeling that he was going to find out something useful to make it easy to trace his real father.

Dr Mehta was scrutinising him, and seeing the look of expectation on this young man's face, he said, "You are a replica of my old mate, except for a smile in his eyes and a moustache that he was so proud of. You have most of his looks: the height and the crop on your head, especially the lock of hair that keeps playing around your eyes. You throw your head up to blow it away. What a coincidence! But sad to say, he was an English doctor."

"That's what I want to know, sir." Vickram began to shower him with questions. "What was the name of this doctor? Where did you meet him?"

Dr Mehta was taken aback. Then collecting his wits, he guessed that there was some sort of mystery about this young man.

"It was a long time ago. Just before the war, I was appointed as an assistant junior doctor at Mathenge Hospital, one of the oldest hospitals in Nairobi. Apart from European doctors, there were a number of Indian doctors working in and Nairobi.

"Anyway, most of the doctors had been given bungalows on the outskirts of the town. There were green fields in the surrounding area where we used to play golf on Sundays. My bungalow was next to this doctor's. My wife got friendly with the doctor's housemaid. As she was an Indian, my wife used to treat her like family. We also found out why she got the job with the doctor. She had been educated at a convent school while she was in India, and that's why she could speak fluent English.

"We used to think that because the maid was pretty and possessed all the qualities a good wife should have, he could have easily married her. But alas, he was not the marrying kind. Yet it was obvious from the maid's behaviour that she thought the world of her employer."

Vickram was listening to him as if he were a child hearing a fairy tale. He could imagine this housemaid whose face appeared in front of his eyes. His mother's smiling face was looking at him. Her earlier pictures showed that she must have been very beautiful. He wanted this elderly doctor to go on relating more about her.

"But, sir, you haven't told me the name of this doctor and his housemaid."

"Sorry, son, but why are you so interested in them? By the way, you haven't told me your name yet!"

Vickram sat up straight. He looked Dr Mehta straight in the face. He looked like his father, so humble and serene. He decided to spill the beans to this stranger.

"Well, destiny makes us its puppets, and we dance accordingly. This destiny has brought me all the way from Kenya to Uganda. My name is Vickram. I am also a doctor—Dr Vickram Patel. My father's name is Girish Patel, and he's a retail salesman in Nairobi.

"About three years ago, I had thought myself a very lucky man. I had a doting mother, a father, and two siblings. When I came back home after graduating from Edinburgh University, with my MBBS degree, my father was pleased that I had gotten a place in one of the top hospitals in Nairobi to do an internship for the first year. I had a plan to go back after some time to complete specialising as a children's doctor.

"That was my dream, to become a fully qualified paediatrician, for I love little children. My father had promised to help me with my own clinic for children. But due to my mother's frail health, I had to put this wish at the back of my mind.

"My mother fell ill, and day by day, her condition started going downhill. My father hadn't told me in the beginning about the real problem with her deteriorating health. By the time I came to know, it was too late to do anything. Even going for the last option, to have an operation, wouldn't have helped. My mother breathed her last in my arms. The irony of the situation was that if she had passed away just like that, I would have come to terms with life as it was.

"The worst blow destiny gave to me was that before breathing for the last time, she mumbled something in my ear. The effect was devastating. I felt as if someone were hitting me with a ton of bricks! The shocking revelation made me a complete stranger. I learned that Girish Patel is not my real father..."

Dr Mehta didn't say anything. He knew that the poor boy had been keeping the knowledge within his heart, torturing himself but not daring to let anyone know the truth. He knew that Vickram had come to the limit of tolerance and wanted to break his silence.

"It's surprising, sir, that you are the first person I am telling all this. Maybe I feel safe because you are a stranger and there is no threat to my reputation from you. Anyway, when you said that I looked like someone you knew years ago, I felt such a relief which I cannot express. Because you see, my biological father happens to be an English doctor! I also knew that he had left Nairobi to come to Uganda.

"When a team of doctors was appointed to work at Mulago Hospital in Kampala, I jumped at the chance. My father couldn't understand why I wanted to go so far. He didn't know that since my mother's death, I had been busy trying to find out from the hospital records about any English doctors who had left Nairobi to go to Kampala."

Dr Mehta exclaimed in excitement, "I remember now why he had to leave Nairobi, Vickram! The MO had offered a job with a higher salary if he agreed to accept the offer of a senior doctor in the medical ward of one of the old hospitals in Kampala. I'll tell you what had happened.

"After he accepted the offer, all of us doctors decided to give him a farewell party. After the party, he left Nairobi within a week. My wife was a bit upset because the maid had disappeared the day after the party. My wife had been planning to give the job to her after the doctor left. I've forgotten the name of that maid. The only thing I remember about her is that she came from a Gujrati background; that's why she became so close to my family. She was a well-to-do young lady, even in those days, when most of our women were denied the right to read and write."

"Yes, Dr Mehta! She was a well-to-do woman, and she was my mother!"

Dr Mehta was baffled. His mouth opened, but no sound came out. It was as if his throat had gotten stuck.

"You got a shock, didn't you? You can understand now why I left home to find out about this doctor who had left my mother in a ditch."

"I am sorry to hear that, Vickram. I have no right to interfere in your life, but believe me, there must have been a genuine reason for the doctor to desert your mother. If she had left his employment before he left Nairobi, maybe she didn't want to keep in touch with him afterwards. He was a lovable doctor, very popular in the days when he was working in Nairobi. But, Vickram, it could be that your mother had genuine feelings for him and he never knew about that!

"I remember that my wife used to like the maid very much. They used to exchange many recipes for different dishes. Your mother was gifted with the culinary arts. She used to love cooking, and as my wife used to say, only a woman in love would do that for the man in her life."

"Do you think that I have been unreasonable for not telling my dad the real reason for coming to Kampala?"

Dr Mehta took off his glasses and took a good look at this young doctor. He was right. He looked like his father. It also made sense why he had the doctor's body frame but his mother's features. The colouring was mixed. His eyes were totally like his father's.

"Where are you staying at the moment, Dr Vickram?"

Vickram was getting slightly impatient because Dr Mehta was dodging the issue and was not telling the name of the doctor.

"Please, sir, can you tell me the name of that doctor? Do tell me if you know—it's vitally important."

"I do apologise for not telling you his full name, but to tell you the truth, we all used to call him Dr John Nicholas. We never bothered to find out his full name because there wasn't any need for that. We used to call each other by our first names. He was John; I was Ravi, short for Ravinder; and there was another doctor whom we called Doug, short for Douglas. I remember that his surname was a long one, but we never bothered to find out about it."

"That information I already acquired from one of the old hospital files, sir. I'm still in the dark about the identity of my biological father."

Dr Mehta was saddened by the sad tone of Vickram's voice. Before getting up to go, he shook Vickram's hand.

"If you don't mind, Vickram, can I have your contact number to keep in touch with you? In case I happen to find out his surname . . . Maybe I'll run into someone who been working in the same hospital where we were before John went away."

"Thank you, sir. I'd appreciate that very much. I'll give you the number of my home in Nairobi because I will be going back home in a week's time. Actually, I had also come to say goodbye to someone dear to my heart. Just like yourself."

They parted company in a friendly way.

Vickram looked at his watch. It was getting late, he thought, and he decided to drive straight to Gulu. The flight to London was going to take off at any moment. He could visualise Tanya sitting next to the window and looking out. Could she be looking for him, just to say goodbye with a smile?

The feeling of loneliness was creeping slowly over him as he got in the car. A moment later, he was surprised to see Captain Hussain coming towards the car park. Vickram decided to drive ahead of the captain. He thought that if he could drive at a steady speed, he'd be able to reach Gulu in a couple of hours.

The sound of the aircraft taking off held him spellbound for a moment. Then he pushed the accelerator, and within a moment, he was on his way towards Gulu. While driving, he could see the blinking lights of the plane.

Farewell, Tanya. We will meet soon!

CHAPTER 14

By the time Captain Hussain got in his jeep, Vickram's car had disappeared in the darkness of the night. For a while, he felt overtaken by fatigue, but he quickly controlled himself. There was a bottle of Coke near him. He grabbed it and emptied it all at once.

This wasn't the first time that he'd had to drive in the middle of the night. He even enjoyed driving in the dark, as there was less stress because there weren't so many vehicles on the road. He was glad that he had sent Nargis back in his family car. She wanted to see Tanya and Manjit, and after saying her farewell, there was no need for her to stay this late.

He was going over the sad scene he had witnessed earlier. When he was about to turn back after saying his farewell to Bobby and Manjit, he had caught Tanya and Vickram holding hands and just looking at each other without blinking their eyes. Not a word was exchanged. When

Vickran tried to hold back her face to make her say something, she still was like a statue. It was only when the other passengers urged her to move ahead that she moved. Vickram was staring at her back while she slowly disappeared with the rest of the crowd going through the gate.

He had felt so sorry for Vickram at that moment that even his throat had become choked when he saw the miserable look on his face. That was why he had decided to keep a watch on the doctor, for driving with a distressed mind was not safe for anybody.

They had left Entebbe far behind. If they drove steadily like this, then they'd reach Gulu within a couple of hours. Now and then, Vickram's car would pick up speed, and Hussain had to do the same. He didn't want to lose sight of Vickram's car.

All of a sudden, he saw an army truck coming quickly towards them. The road wasn't wide enough for it to pass Vickram's car without hitting it. The car couldn't take the sudden blow of the oncoming slaughter and went out of control.

Hussain braked sharply, and before he could shout for the truck driver to stop, he just drove on and disappeared like a flash of light in the darkness of the night. He made a note of the time the truck had driven past so that he'd be able to confront the ruthless driver. But for the time being, his concern was for Vickram. What he saw brought his heart to his mouth.

He was glad that he had decided to follow Vickram or else he would have bled to death lying in the wreckage of his car. All he knew was that he had to get the doctor out of the car and take him to the nearest hospital as soon as possible. He had come across accident victims while doing his duty at the barracks, but seeing someone who was known to him was extremely difficult to bear.

It took him some time before he could free Vickram from the broken debris that had trapped him. Besides the shattered pieces of the windscreen glass, some broken metal pieces of the windowpanes had bruised his neck and forehead. His body had been lying on top of the steering wheel after hitting the windscreen. He was dreading the fact that some inner injuries could have occurred as well. At the moment, the blood that was gushing from his head was the priority to attend to first. He looked around to see if there was any piece of cloth or even a hand towel in the car so that he could tie it around his head.

He caught sight of a white handkerchief in the top coat pocket. He took it out and quickly tied it around Vickran's forehead. That would at least cover the lower part of the head wound. After lying the injured doctor on the back seat of the jeep, he looked around to see which way was the quickest route to the hospital. Kampala was not very far, so the best thing was to take him to Mulago Hospital. He knew that Vickram had worked in that hospital for some time, so it would be easy to get quick treatment.

Eventually, when Hussain brought Vickram into the hospital reception area, there was hardly anyone around. There was no one behind the reception desk either. He had already placed Vickram on a stretcher that was lying near the entrance door. He looked around and could see people moving through the windows, but no one was within his reach.

He went to the bell on the reception desk and pressed hard and continuously until he heard footsteps running towards him.

A couple of nurses and a porter appeared in front of him. They must have seen the uniform-clad officer.

"Sorry to keep you waiting, sir. Can we help you?"

Hussain didn't say anything, He pointed at the stretcher. Within minutes, a number of doctors appeared there. Vickram was taken to the casualty quickly. Nobody asked any questions.

One of the doctors came over to talk to Hussain after a while. He had been waiting for Vickram to regain consciousness. One of the nurses had offered a cup of tea, which he refused. He had to know how bad the injuries were. When he saw the doctor coming towards him, he asked him quickly about Vickram.

"That was a big shock you gave us, sir, because I never expected to see Dr Vickram in this state. How did this happen?"

Hussain explained briefly how the accident had happened. The doctor introduced himself as Dr Joshi. He had known

Vickram ever since he had come to work there. Then when Vickram moved up North, they lost touch.

"Please, Doctor, can you hurry up with the treatment?" Hussain was getting agitated now. He was seized with a fear that Vickram's injuries could be very serious.

The X-ray showed that his collar one was fractured, but it wasn't very bad. There was no damage to the skull, but the deep gash on his head and part of his forehead was the main cause of the loss of blood.

It was surprising that all of a sudden, a team of doctors had appeared to help with the treatment. Hussain knew that the magic of his uniform had alerted everyone at the hospital.

In spite of being one of the largest hospitals in Uganda, Mulago Hospital continued to look deserted. It could be due to the expulsion that a majority of patients and nurses had left the country by now. He was thinking that it would take a while to recruit new staff for the already existing patients.

He was sitting in the waiting room having tea and something to eat. The doctors had already told him that they had been trying their best to find the right type of blood so an operation could be performed as soon as possible. He was thinking of letting Vicram's father know about the accident. Maybe his blood group could match Vickram's.

The worrying thing was that because of weakness in the immune system, the operation was not possible. He decided to phone Lacor Hospital as well. Suddenly, he got up. He'd forgotten to phone Dr Kimberley about the accident. He could try to find the right blood for Vickram.

After phoning Lacor, he went to see Vickram. He was devastated to see him like this. He felt so helpless that he could do nothing to get the doctor back on his feet.

Time was running out. There was no sign of Dr Kimberley or Girish Patel. He was sitting in the waiting area with his mind far away. Someone touched his shoulder.

Dr Joshi was looking at him. "I was thinking, sir, that while we are searching for the right type of blood, perhaps you could let Vickram's father know about the accident and the need for blood as well? He's in Nairobi. I'm sure we can find the contact number in Vickram's wallet or from something else in his pocket."

"I'm glad that you reminded me about this. I have been thinking of phoning Nairobi, but I was waiting for Dr Kimberley, thinking he might have the contact number of Girish Patel. It didn't occur to me that Vickram could have the number. Come on, then!" Hussain jumped up from the chair.

"We shouldn't waste any more time," he was saying a moment later. "Can you check Vickram's trouser pocket or his jacket and let me have his wallet?"

Dr Joshi had placed Vickram's belongings in a locker when he was brought in for the operation. He took out the wallet and took it straight to the captain.

• THE SECRET OF ANU •

Hussain opened the wallet, and his eyes fell on a photograph of an attractive young woman. Surprisingly, she had an old-fashioned Indian look, with dark hair styled with a parting in the middle and tied at the nape of her neck in the shape of a bun. Her almond-shaped eyes were half closed. He felt as if he were looking at an old Indian painting of a beautiful woman he had seen a long time ago but couldn't remember where.

His eyes narrowed when he realised that he had expected the picture to be of Tanya, Vickram's sweetheart! He shrugged his shoulders, thinking that it was none of his business.

After shuffling through the contents in the wallet, he came across a small card that had Mr Girish Patel's number and the address of his home and business. He felt relieved that he could contact him now.

Girish Patel was shocked when he came to know about his son's accident. He couldn't believe it at first, because he was expecting Vickram to phone him that he was coming back home.

He didn't waste time, especially when he learned that the hospital didn't have the blood to match Vickram's blood. It was of a rare group. He called his driver to get the car ready. It was a long journey and would take almost all day without stopping on the way.

Before getting in the car, he phoned Mulago Hospital, informing them about his plans. He was glad that an experienced driver who had taken part in the East African Safari Rally was driving him.

Back at the hospital, Dr Mathew was waiting for Dr Kimberley to arrive at any minute. It had been more than two hours since he was informed about the accident. He looked at his watch and was about to call the captain when he saw someone coming hurriedly towards the reception desk. He knew the wait was over. Dr Kimberley had arrived with Carol at his heels.

Alice Bigombe, one of the senior nurses, came forward to greet them. After a formal introduction, Dr Kimberley said, "Nurse, is Vickram in the operating theatre?"

"Yes, sir. I think Captain Hussain knows more about this case," she replied. She had seen the captain coming towards them.

"I'm glad to see you, Dr Kimberley," the captain said. "I feel relieved that there's someone to take care of Vickram. Dr Mathews is the surgeon in charge. I was waiting for your arrival, and now I must go resume my duty. But I will keep in touch to learn about Vickram's progress."

Dr Kimberley shook his hand. "Thanks a lot for getting Vickram to the hospital and being with him when nobody else was here to help him. Dr Joshi told me that you'd witnessed the accident and were able to give a helping hand. We are lucky to have someone like you with us during these troubled times." His voice had become heavy with compassion.

The captain felt the emotion as well. He looked at Carol, who was standing quietly to one side. "I'll take you to see Vickram, Mrs Kimberley. Your husband has to see the doctor who is going to operate Vickram's injured collarbone." He marched ahead, Carol following him.

She was heartbroken to see Vickram in this state. Her head was full of questions. Why did this have happen when everyone had left the country! On the other hand, his father must be waiting for him in Nairobi. She wished that they could have stopped Vickram from following Tanya. He should have made his way to Nairobi and applied for a visa straight away.

But in every aspect of life, destiny always has surprises for mankind.

When John came to know about Vickram's blood group, he threw his hands up in exasperation. "Why don't you get on with your work, Doctor? Time is running out, and the operation should be performed immediately!"

"But the blood . . . ?"

"Dr Mathews, Nurse Alice, please do not worry about the blood. You just get the patient ready for the operation."

Dr Mathews was the surgeon who had been called to perform the operation. Three hours had passed since the accident. The doctors and nurses had done all they could do to treat his injuries that were visible, but he still hadn't regained consciousness. A lot of blood had been lost after the accident, and even though the bleeding had been stopped, there wasn't enough supply going to the brain.

Within a few minutes, the operation was being performed. They now had enough blood for the transfusion for the operation to go on without a hitch.

Alice had seen a plaster on Dr Kimberley's arm and put two and two together. Her guess was right. Dr Kimberley had given his blood to the patient. Dr Mathews was washing his hands in the washbasin after performing the operation, and when she mentioned the plaster tape on Dr Kimberley's arm, he smiled and said, "I am really surprised how Dr Kimberley managed to have everything under control so quickly and efficiently. Did you know, Nurse, why he was saying not to worry about the blood? Because he was the blood donor. The conniving devil! I am glad that Dr Vickram will be all right by the grace of God, or shall I say Dr Kimberley!"

Nurse Alice nodded in agreement. "I do believe that it was the will of God for Vickram to get better. For a little while, we were really in a panic when we couldn't get any donor coming forth with the right blood. I'm still confused, though. Vickram looks so much like Dr Kimberley, who is a thorough Englishman, while Vickram is Indian."

"Only half Indian, if my guess is right."

Startled, both of them turned to stare at the newcomer who had just spoken those shocking words. An elderly Indian gentleman was coming towards them. Before Dr Mathews could say anything, the man put out his hand in greeting.

"I'm sorry to come barging in like this. I'm Girish Patel, Vickram's father. I was looking for the surgeon who performed the operation on my son, Vickram. I was told that I would find him here."

Dr Mathews shook his hand. "You've found him, Mr Patel. I'm Dr Mathews. I'm glad that you made it in good time. We wanted to wait for you before we proceeded with the formalities before an operation of any kind. Luckily, Dr Kimberley signed the forms, taking all the responsibility of Vickram on his shoulders. By the way, why did you say that Vickram is half Indian?"

Girish laughed, and without explaining properly about his outburst, he went out towards the recovery room. He wanted to spend as much time as possible with his son. There had been a burden on him since his wife had died. He wished that the truth could have come out while she was alive. But she had made him swear that he'd never tell Vickram about his real identity.

He felt wretched and miserable seeing his son lying on the hospital bed. Vickram was still unconscious. He would be kept in the recovery room until the effect of the morphine wore off. Girish had learned that it hasn't been long since the operation. It would take some time before he was fully awake. He decided to sit by the bedside and wait for Vickram to open his eyes.

Dr Kimberley came to take him to the waiting room. He knew that Girish had had a long journey and needed rest and something to eat. He had been travelling without stopping on the way.

"As soon as Vickram is awake, we'll inform you immediately. Please have some rest so you will look fresh and fit to face your son. You don't want him to get worried when he awakens and sees the dishevelled face of his dad, right?"

Leaving Girish with the nurse, Dr Kimberley went out to join Dr Mathews in the reception area. The doctor was sitting there chatting with Carol, who had thrown her head back and was laughing at something he had been telling her.

There were still not many people around, but it was early. The doctors usually started their duties after ten in the morning. There were few nurses about with medicine trollies, going towards the wards.

All of a sudden, the reception area filled with more emergency cases waiting to be admitted in the casualty department. Dr Mathews took him towards his office, where they could sit without being disturbed.

"One thing I can't understand, Doctor, is how you knew about Vickram's blood group. We were waiting for Mr Girish to help us!"

"It wasn't so difficult. As soon as Captain Hussain told me about the need for more blood, I went to see Vickram's record card at Lacor Hospital. I got a shock when I found out that his blood group matched mine! So without wasting any more time, I quickly picked up Carol from home. Captain Hussain phoned the army headquarters in Gulu to send an escort with us, so we should not face any delay by the security forces on the way." John looked at Dr Mathews closely. He had a feeling that the surgeon wanted to ask him something but was hesitating.

"Dr Mathews, is there something you want to tell me? I can see a question in your eyes." John himself was filled with unanswered questions.

"I'm not sure if it's of any importance to you. Captain Hussain saw a picture in Vickram's wallet, and according to him, the face in the picture wasn't of the girl he was going to marry. I think the captain was worried because Vickram's fiancée and his wife had been close friends."

"Now you have made me worried too, Dr Mathews! Tanya has been like a daughter to Carol too. Look, is it possible to get Vickram's wallet? Maybe there's a valid reason for another woman's picture being in it."

Dr Mathews got up and was back within a few minutes. The wallet had still been in the locker. He only had to look for Dr Joshi to open the locker. He handed the wallet to John and went out again. One of the nurses had called him.

John was looking at the open wallet. His eyes glued to what he was seeing. It may have been a long time—more than thirty years since he'd seen her for the last time—but his last meeting with her had left a deep impression in his mind. How could he forget that serene-looking face! Those haunting eyes had always disturbed his peace of mind. Like a distant horizon, her vision had constantly appeared whenever he had thought about her.

What was her picture doing in Vickram's wallet? He suddenly sat upright. His heart was beating with the sudden revelation. Was Vickram his son? The naked truth was staring at him. How could he have forgotten that fateful night when he had come home half-drunk from his farewell party? It seemed like an eternity since that night!

The party given by the hospital staff had gone very well. It was nearly midnight when he had called a taxi to take him home. He wanted to get away quickly before he made a nuisance of himself. Some of the nurses were openly flirting with him. One of them had even thrown herself in his arms, and he had difficulty breaking free.

"Dr Kimberley, with your handsome looks and dashing personality, you could have easily gotten hooked by now. At least we could have a good time for the time being?"

John was becoming attracted towards Nurse Finchley, who had been eyeing him for a long time. Before his self-control gave way, he decided to go home quickly. He was confused because all of a sudden, he felt uneasy. It was difficult to control feelings of desire for a woman. He was human, after all, but he had vowed that he's never play with any girl's feelings. The only person he had been close to was Dr Mary Wilson.

Anyway, he was leaving this place for good. One day he would decide to settle down. Maybe, while in Kampala, he'd meet his future partner. His mind full of these thoughts, he opened the front door of his house.

There was a light on in the hallway. He was surprised to see that a light was still on in the lounge as well. He was not steady on his feet, and slowly he went towards the sofa, where the maid was sleeping. For one moment, his eyes were stuck on her.

"Ani . . . Miss Lakhaaniii," he babbled, and before he could go on, the maid jumped up, looking terrified.

"I am sorry, Sahib. Kamau had to go home to see to his sick mother, and that's why I am still here waiting for you!" She looked apologetically towards her employer. "If there is something you want before going to bed, I'll get it for you before going to my abode."

John dropped on the nearest sofa chair. He could hardly stand on his feet. He saw her worried look, and with a big grin, he said, "Come here, Ani. Sit on this chair." He was quiet for some time as if thinking what to say. "Actually, I forgot to tell you that I will be leaving this place in a few days. I have a great job in a hospital in Kampala. I'm sorry that I waited so long to inform you. I should have told you earlier because you'll have to find another job now. Don't worry. I will give you a very good referral letter to help you find another job."

He was shocked to see her reaction. She came towards him and fell at his feet. She looked up at him with eyes full of unshed tears. "Sahib! You don't mean to leave this place for good?"

He was puzzled by her reaction. Then, at the back of his mind, he started to remember numerous incidents. There were moments when she was serving dinner that he had caught Ani looking at him with longing in her eyes; then she would look away quickly. Then there was the time when Kamau had told her about his birthday. She had prepared a lavish meal for him that day. It wasn't only the spread on the table but a birthday cake as well. To complete the picture, she had invited one of the neighbours to join them, a surprise for John. He hadn't expected anyone else to join them that day. But it turned out to be one of the most memorable moments in his life since leaving home back in England.

That day, Ani had taken off her apron and her cap. She had put on one of her best dresses that had made her look quite pretty. But then, she was a beautiful woman. Her only problem was that she preferred to keep her looks hidden under her frilly cap that was always falling over her forehead. The natural texture of her complexion didn't need any make-up, as there was always a glow on her face He looked at her bowed head, and some sort of compassion took hold of him. He bent down to lift her up to her feet. He had never expected her to react like this. Oh dear! She seemed to be smitten by him, and that wasn't good.

For a little while, they stood like that. Then as if some unforeseen force were pushing her towards him, she threw her arms around him and clung to him as if by holding him, she'd be able to stop him from going away.

"Dr Sahib, I know you'll go away from here and I'll never see you again. So can I ask you to do me a favour, please?"

"Of course you can. Just ask for whatever you have in mind, Ani! I am in a generous mood," John murmured slowly. He could hear only a whisper coming from her mouth.

"I want to cherish this moment. I want you to give me something as a memento, to remember you in your absence."

He was thoughtful for a long moment. He knew that Ani was extremely naive and wanted something that he had in his possession. He looked deep in her eyes. All of a sudden, his whole being was taken over by a deep desire that a man feels for a woman. And he was a man, after all, and he also had desires hidden within himself.

Without thinking anymore, he lifted Ani up in his arms and went towards his bedroom. For him, these may have been snatched moments to satisfy his sexual desire. He also knew that for a woman like Ani, it was going to be cherished memory for the rest of her life. He had known for some time that she had started to care for him very much. He had felt attraction for her now and then, but he wasn't ready to tie himself with any responsibility apart from his work as a doctor, which was to serve mankind.

There was a knock on the door, and the next minute, the duty nurse came in to get some files from the desk. John got up to go see how Vickram was.

His mind was still numb. If Vickram was Ani's son, then it was obvious that he—John Kimberley—could be his biological father!

Chapter 15

Vickram was moved to a private room with plenty of light. With half-open eyes, he tried hard to think clearly where he was. He couldn't fathom properly, as his head was hurting so much.

He touched his head and felt a bandage tied there. There was another bandage covering his neck and upper part of his chest. Everything around him was white. The room was white, and the bedsheets were white too. There were some figures moving around, and they were white as well. He blinked his eyes and saw more clearly. He was lying in a bed. It slowly dawned on him that he was actually in a hospital. That explained all the white around him. The white shadows were the doctors and nurses.

Seeing that his eyes were open, one of the nurses exclaimed, "Doctor, he is coming round!" Within seconds, someone had lifted his arm to check his pulse.

"Thank God you are all right, son! You gave us such a fright that for a while, we thought you had stopped breathing." The kind face of the doctor was looking down at him.

"I am all right, Doctor, but I have a terrible headache. What happened? Where am I?" He tried to get up, but the doctor made him lie back again.

"Please try to rest, Dr Vickram. You are not in a state to move around yet. You are still in the recovery room of Mulago Hospital. You may not remember, but due to the accident, you damaged your collarbone. We had to perform an emergency operation to treat it."

Vickram closed his eyes and tried to think how the accident had happened. He couldn't recall anything at the moment except some nightmare he had been going through. All he could remember was seeing a vast sea everywhere. He was being taken by the waves towards a big hole in the middle of the ocean. His cries had vanished in the terrible sound of the sea storm. Then all of a sudden, someone pulled him back. The next minute he saw that his father was holding him with his arms wrapped around him tightly. The face was supposed to be his father's, but it was blurred. He was wondering about the significance of those visions.

His headache was getting really bad. The bandage on his head must be due to his head injury. He relaxed, thinking that head injuries are prone to cause these nightmares. He could hear the doctor telling the nurse that the effect of the sedative was still there and he was not to be disturbed. He dozed off soon after that.

It was much later that Vickram was shifted to a private room. He was asleep, but his mind was still far from being clear. He slept for a long time. Outside his room, life was still going on in the busy hospital. The duty nurse had opened the door a little to see if he was still asleep.

He was fully awake now but didn't want to open his eyes yet. His thoughts had wandered away. He was with Tanya just before she left Gulu. There was one particular moment that came suddenly to his mind.

It was late afternoon on a Sunday. Tanya had come to get some of her files from Aggarwal's office. He had already left and had told Tanya to hand the keys of the office to Dr Kimberley. As Vickram was still in the flat, he couldn't lock it up and surrender the keys to the DC of Gulu District. Dr Kimberley was going to look after the keys meanwhile. Vickram was surprised to see her standing outside the door when he opened it.

"Tanya, it's naughty of you to show up like this. I could have been in the bathroom and unable to open the door for you!"

Tanya didn't answer him. Instead, she wound her arms around him, and looking up at his unshaven beard, she burst out laughing. "You look like one of those bandits in the western movies. Go on and finish your tasks in the bathroom, Vickram. I'll wait for you and make tea for you while I do."

Tanya had come unexpectedly. He could have finished his personal washing-up ages ago, but because it was his off day, he wanted to relax and chill out. But he obeyed Tanya's command and was quick to freshen up.

He came out of the bathroom wearing his linen slacks and a vest. It was hot, and he wanted to feel cool. He stood watching Tanya pour the tea in two cups.

"Tanya, please leave the teacups in the tray and come over and help me." He went towards his bedroom. Tanya followed him, looking puzzled.

"Tanya, I want you to lift up my vest from my back. See if there is a bruise of a mosquito bite. I've been feeling itchy and uncomfortable. My hand won't reach the spot."

"Okay, Vickram. Just sit on the bed so that I can check it for you. You are so tall that my eyes won't be able to see the trouble spot clearly."

Vickram sat down on the bed. Tanya bent down and lifted the vest up from his bare back. Suddenly, he felt her hands moving all over his back. He was feeling a tickling sensation but was enjoying her soft touch on his bare skin. He let her caress his bare back for a while and started to feel some excitement.

"What are you doing Tanya? You're tickling me!"

"I don't know, Vickram, but I like the touch of flesh. I feel like caressing it with my mouth." Saying this, she started to rub her face against his back, and in between she gave him kisses as well. It was too much for Vickram. He wasn't so naive that he didn't understand what she was getting up to. He turned his back suddenly and faced her, giving her a piercing look.

"You're asking for this Tanya." The next minute, he had wrapped up her trembling body in the fold of his arms. She had closed her eyes as if knowing what was going to happen. He knew at that moment that she did not intend to get out of his hold at all. In the end, even he let go of any inhibitions that may have been bothering him in the past.

He opened his eyes and saw the nurse looking down at him. She was smiling while taking his temperature. "It's nice to see you getting better, sir. Your eyes were closed, yet you were mumbling something."

"I am feeling a bit better, except for this terrible headache. Nurse, can you give me a painkiller to get rid of this pain?"

As the nurse gave him a tablet and handed him a glass of water, she told him that his father was waiting to see him. Vickram wasn't in a mood to talk to anyone at the moment. He told the nurse to tell everyone that he would see them in the morning, when he'd be feeling much better.

"Please close the door behind you. I want to sleep." He fell asleep soon after that. This time he went into a deep sleep, maybe due to the effect of the medicine.

Two days had passed since his accident. As the deadline was approaching quickly, most of the Asian people had left Uganda. Dr Kimberley had gone back to Gulu with Carol. They were needed back at Lacor due to the current shortage of hospital staff.

He didn't tell Carol the truth about Vickram. He couldn't even bring himself to tell Vickram that his mother used to work for him when he was in Nairobi.

He had felt guilty in the presence of Girish Patel. Actually, he was surprised that Girish had given him a scrutinising look when they shook hands at their first meeting. John himself hadn't told anyone about his part in donating blood for Vickram. He had made Nurse Alice Bigombe promise to keep it a secret. He knew he could trust her, but he wasn't sure about Dr Mathews, who was bound to find out from the nurse one of these days.

He didn't know that Dr Mathews was a step ahead of him. He had figured it out, and while John was away in Gulu, he planned to have a serious talk with Girish Patel.

"By the way, Mr Patel, I have something to tell you. When you are free, please come to my consulting room in the afternoon after four o'clock. I will be free then."

"Sure, Doctor. I'll come after seeing my son first." Girish was relieved that the surgeon was going to enlighten him as to Vickram's progress. He wanted to take his son away from the present environment. He couldn't wait for the doctor to tell him that Vickram was making steady progress and could go with him home now.

At exactly four, he knocked on the door that had a nameplate reading Dr Mathews. It was well past six when the door opened and Girish Patel came out. Whatever their talk had involved, it seemed both of them were pleased with the outcome of it.

Dr Mathews had ordered two cups of tea so they could relax and talk. "Something the British have given us as a legacy!"

"What's that, sir?"

"A cup of tea!" He threw back his head and laughed at his own statement.

Girish also smiled. "You're right, Doctor. Tea has become an important part of our daily life."

"I'm joking, Mr Patel. Being a doctor, I shouldn't encourage any intake of caffeine. Still, it is our weakness which we can overcome if need be."

Dr Mathew was from Kenya. He had belonged to the Leo tribe from Kisumu. He had completed his education at Makerere University. He had to go abroad to specialise as a surgeon. Mulago Hospital had given him a good chance to establish his skill.

Girish Patel opened the door a little to see if Vickram was still asleep. He had sat with his son yesterday when he had looked fit to talk to. He knew that it wasn't the effect of the operation that was making Vickram lethargic and lost in his thoughts. He was sure that some inner turmoil was making his son restless. He wanted to find out what was bothering him so much that he had forgotten to smile.

The nurse had just finished taking his temperature and blood pressure. When she saw Girish at the door, she smiled at him and said, "I am glad to say that Dr Vickram is much better now. His blood pressure is normal, and the temperature has gone down a little. It's puzzling us why he's still feverish. Anyway, Dr Mathew will see him afterwards."

After seeing that Girish had taken a seat next to the bed, she went out, closing the door gently. It was nice to see that the young doctor had someone of his own to talk to. Thinking about Vickram, she smiled and walked towards the next patient waiting for her attention.

It had been four years since Vickram had left Nairobi. It was only during his annual holidays that he spent time with his father, who also made sure that he was home during that time. It was during one of his visits that Vickram told his father about Tanya. But he hadn't yet told him that he had already gotten engaged to be married sometime in the near future.

Girish Patel was looking forward to meeting his future daughter-in-law. He was very disappointed to find out that Tanya had gone to England with her folks. He couldn't understand why Vickram had let her go at all!

He had been waiting for Vickram's recovery, to ask him for any explanation if there was one. As far as he was concerned, his son could have gotten married in a registrar's office. That would have stopped Tanya from taking such a drastic step. He knew that Tanya's people were not old-fashioned, but being Indian, some limits were not to be crossed. They wouldn't have left Tanya left behind without first giving her hand in marriage to Vickram.

Vickram was looking at his father. His heart filled with compassion for this dear man who had always stood by him through thick and thin. Like a metal shield, his father had protected him from any calamity that had engulfed him when he was growing up.

He clung to his father, his voice almost at a breaking point. "I have missed you, Papa. I'm so sorry for leaving you alone after Mama died..."

He held Vickram away from him by the shoulders, trying to sound cheerful. "You don't have to feel sorry, my dear, because somewhere in the back of my head, I knew that you got wind of the truth about your identity."

"I could see the sudden change that came over you after Anu breathed her last breath in your arms. At first, I put your restlessness to the loss of your mother. But when I realised that you were very serious about going to Uganda, I figured out what had happened. I knew that if Anu had revealed that some doctor was your biological father, then you'd be itching to find out about him. You see, Vickram, I already knew that he had gone to Kampala."

"Hey, wait a minute, Papa! You're saying that you knew all along who was my real father! That means it wasn't a secret as I had been led to believe?"

"Meaning?"

"I just assumed it was a secret, hence Mama telling me about it when she had realised that she had very little time left to live."

"Actually, Vickram, it was my suggestion to your mama that you'd never come to know that I was not your father. I wanted you to call me Papa. There was magic in that word. I was only your papa, and that's why the twins call me Daddy."

This was one of those rare moments shared by two when the outside world ceased to exist for them.

"Papa, can I ask you something about Mama?"

"Of course, son. You don't have to ask me. Just say whatever is in your heart."

Vickram was quiet for a little while and then suddenly looked straight in his father's eyes, saying in a low voice, "How did you meet Mama?"

Girish was taken aback. He hadn't expected such a blatant question from Vickram. He looked at his son with a straight face, but soon a smile started playing around his face.

He sat down with his back resting against the back of the chair. His eyes had a faraway look in them when he started to talk.

"It seems as if it happened only yesterday. I was waiting to meet a client, to make a very important business deal. We had arranged to meet in a hotel which was situated in the heart of Nairobi and was convenient for entertainment as well.

"The meeting was brief but successful. After my client left, I went to the lobby and sat down, waiting for my driver. There was still half an hour left, so to pass the time, I started to read the newspaper. Without lifting my head from the paper, I sensed that someone had come to sit on the chair opposite me.

"I lowered the paper a little to satisfy my curiosity. I was surprised to see a young Indian girl, and she appeared to be in her early twenties. She was sitting there all alone, looking at the people coming in and going out of the hotel. It's not her being alone that raised my curiosity. It was because the hotel wasn't a reputed one. There were all sorts of characters lurking about the place. In fact, it wasn't safe place for a young girl to be wandering alone. Suddenly, I had a bout of a nasty cough. I put the paper to one side, with my other hand covering my mouth.

"'Here, sir, drink some water. Your throat is dry—that's why this cough . . .'"

"I looked up, and my eyes met two of the loveliest eyes I had ever seen. Actually, Vickram, you have your mother's eyes except the colouring. Have you ever noticed that?"

"Oh yeah, Papa. Tanya was always complimenting them. But then, she too has the most beautiful eyes, which was what hooked me in the first place."

"Ah, Tanya! The love of your life . . . Trust you to let her go away to England. Dr Kimberley had told me everything about her."

"I'll tell you all about her later. Now, Papa, don't dodge the issue. You were telling me about Mama. I know she was a beautiful woman and that you met her in the lobby of a hotel. Then what?"

Girish was quiet for a moment. He was back in the past.

"I took the glass of water from her hand and felt relieved that after emptying the glass of water in one gulp, my cough did cease. I thanked her for her kind gesture and asked her the reason for being in that hotel. What she told me filled my heart with sympathy for her.

"She had lost her mother while she was away, studying in a convent school in Ahmadabad, the capital city of Gujrat. Her grandfather was one of Mahatma Gandhi's followers. As he was away from home most of the time, Anu's father had to leave his studies incomplete to look after the family. There came a time when her grandfather was killed in one of the marches. Anu's grandmother and her mother died within a short time of each other.

"One day her father came to collect her from the convent school, telling her that they were travelling to East Africa. An old friend of his had come to see him, with an offer to work with the railway board of Kenya.

"This friend already had a steady job with the railways. There was a big demand for more labourers. As Anu was stepping into adulthood, her father wanted to keep her with him until he could find a suitable boy to marry her.

• THE SECRET OF ANU •

"Things never turn out the way we plan. God always has different plans for mankind. When both of them were well settled in Nairobi, with a secure job and a house to live in comfortably, cruel destiny grabbed their short-lived happiness.

"After completing nearly two years, the railway board promoted her father to a higher rank. His friends gave a party to celebrate his success. When he was coming home after the party, his car collided with an oncoming truck. The car was totally smashed, killing him instantly.

"Anu was all alone in the world. The railways took the house back after her father's death. There was some compensation given to her but no roof over her head. Their family friend gave her shelter for a while until the day his wife threw a fit. She wanted Anu out of the house, saying that a young girl in the house was a threat to her married life.

"One day, the houseboy, who had seen the way Anu was being treated, came to her aid. One of his friends was working for a doctor. There was a need for a good cook as well as an able housekeeper. No need to tell you, Vickram, that Anu had both those qualities. She settled very well in her new environment. The convent education was a blessing for her because she could speak fluent English. Apart from that, she also had a very appealing personality.

"Here also, fate cheated her. She had started to enjoy life in the doctor's household. Their houseboy, who had recommended Anu for the job, was a great company for her. He was only thirteen or fourteen years old and tried very hard to remember the few English words he had learned to communicate with the doctor. He used to speak in Kiswahili most of the time. Anu taught him to read and write. Within a year, he was able to write clearly besides speaking proper English as well.

"She had made friends with the neighbours especially with one of the Indian families. Therefore, when her employer gave her the news that he was leaving Nairobi, she became very upset. Maybe she had started to take it for granted that life was one bed of roses. She forgot that below those flowers lurked thorns that were going to be painful once she walked away from the comfort of the roses.

"Before going to Kampala, the doctor gave her a good reference that could help her get a good job somewhere else. From what Anu told me, I had gathered that she had been getting too close to the doctor. It could have been hero worship or something similar. Because of her fascination with her employer, she became emotionally attached to him.

"She had enough cash on her to spend some time in a hotel and start looking for a job. Well, by now you must have guessed that after listening to her whole story, I offered her the job of a housekeeper. Anyway, she needed a job, and Ba needed a companion because I was away most of the time. My sister had also moved away after she got married.

"Ba loved Anu. They became inseparable in no time. She had hinted many times that I should settle down. The chance came when one day Anu told me that she wanted to leave. I was shocked when she told me the reason for her decision.

"She was pregnant! I was surprised to notice that there was calmness on her face. There was not even a little sign of panic on her face. It seemed as if she was actually happy that she was going to have a baby. Well, I'll never be able to understand a woman. I was in a dilemma. What to do? Should I let her go? Then I thought about Ba, who had become so fond of her, and what about me? I had started to depend on her day by day.

"When I asked her about her previous employer, whatever she told me was enough for me to draw my own conclusion. As I mentioned earlier, she must have thought a lot about him to get herself in that situation. I had already guessed that she wanted to keep the baby. That's why she wanted to leave, so she could go someplace where no one knew her and have the baby quietly.

"After thinking a lot about this predicament, finally I found enough courage and proposed to her. After all, the baby needed a name! I made her promise that she'd never let the baby know the truth. The secret would remain between us."

"I am sorry, Papa, that Mama broke your promise. But she didn't do that while she was alive. On her deathbed, she relieved herself of the guilt of carrying this secret. I hope you'll forgive her now."

He was quiet for some time. His mind was still searching for more answers. "I wish she could have told me his name as well."

Girish wanted to tell him that he had found out the identity of the mysterious doctor. But he kept quiet. Dr Mathews had made him promise not to say anything yet.

"I want to ask you something important, Vickram. It's about Tanya. What happened between you two that she left you to go with her uncle? You have disappointed me. I was looking forward to meet my future daughter-in-law!"

There was no response from Vickram. He was looking down at his bandaged chest. He didn't want his Papa to see that his eyes had become moist with the mention of Tanya's name.

Girish stood up and went to stand close to the bed. Bending down, he lifted his son's head up. He saw the anguish and unshed tears in his eyes. His heart was filled with a surge of love for his son. He folded the shaking body of his son in his arms and let him get rid of all his pent-up emotion.

It was much later when Dr Mathews came to see Vickram. Girish asked him about his son's progress. The stitches wouldn't come out yet, not for another week. The deep gash in the front of his head was the main worry of Dr Mathews. He was puzzled by its prolonged recovery. As far as he was concerned, there was no infection there. From its outer appearance, it just looked like a normal scar that was almost healing now.

He was worried about the headaches that Vickram had been complaining about. In spite of taking painkillers, his patient still hadn't gotten relief from constant headaches. He looked closely at Vickram. There was something brewing in that head of the young doctor. He guessed that the separation from his lady-love was the cause of delay in his progress towards a quick recovery.

Dr Mathews went back to his room. He was thinking about Vickram and Tanya. There had to be some solution to this problem. Thinking he might have found an answer, he quickly got up and picked up the phone.

Chapter 16

Carol was restless. She was puzzled about John's attitude since he came back from Kampala. Since then, he had been frantically getting everything in the house sorted out. Some of the houseboys were helping him pack up big boxes that were to be freighted along with more household furniture.

"Are we leaving Gulu as well, John?" Carol asked. "You haven't even told me about this sudden change of plans." She sounded hurt.

"I am so sorry, Carol. I thought that after everyone left, you wouldn't be able to enjoy even one moment of being alone and always with the fear of an attack by some hooligans, especially kondos and the like. I had to make a quick decision and figured I'd pack up some important items that we cannot take with us on the plane."

"Oh, that's why you have everyone busy with work! I never imagined that you'd ever leave this place, John. By the way, only the Asians have left this place so far. Since when have you started feeling part of the Asian community?"

He wanted to tell her that it was since he had found out that he had a son who was half Indian. Instead, he changed the subject.

"Carol, there was a call from Hussain's wife, Nargis. I forgot to tell you. Sorry for that . . ." He looked sheepish and lowered his face, making it look as if he were very busy.

"Thanks, John," Carol said, shaking her head "I have been waiting for that call since morning time! To tell you the truth, there is something I wanted to tell you, but since you are so engrossed in your present task, I'll wait till you are free to listen."

John looked at Carol in a pleading way. It was funny that he had wanted to tell her something as well, but that he wanted to tell her when he was free of this work at hand.

"Look here, my dear, cook something special for tonight. We'll make it a memorable evening. Afterwards, we can sit and talk over a cup of coffee in the privacy of our room."

That took a load off Carol's mind. She was back to her formal chirpy self. She decided to make that phone call to Hussain's house first. The phone call didn't take that long. She explained to Nargis that they had decided to go to Kampala to see Vickram tomorrow.

"It would be nice if you and Hussain also come with us, Nargis. What Dr Mathews told us is that Mr Girish Patel intends to take Vickram with him back to Nairobi. Vickram's personal things together with his suitcase, which was already packed, was sent to Kampala."

Nargis gave a satisfying answer, and Carol's face was beaming with happiness when she put the receiver back. There was lightness in her steps as she walked towards the kitchen area. She was already planning what to cook for tonight's supper.

It was ages since she had made an effort to pay attention to her appearance. Normally she dressed in a simple skirt and a blouse. Tonight, after finishing her cooking chores, she went to freshen up her appearance.

It was half past seven when Carol came out of her room looking incredibly ravishing, her silvery-golden locks flowing over her face. It was only in the evening that she paid any attention to her appearance. A slight brushing of her hair and powdering of her nose was all she typically had time for.

Today, however, she paid extra attention to her looks. With the help of little make-up, her face was glowing with radiance. The wrinkles had disappeared under the face cream and powder. Her already pink lips didn't need much colour, but she still darkened the shade a bit more. Her white cotton dress with a pink floral print was flowing down to her ankles. With slightly high-heeled shoes, she looked quite tall, reaching up to John's shoulders.

She'd stood in front of the mirror to check how she looked. Her hair was combed, and every curl was in place. The hairstyle was old-fashioned, but there wasn't much choice in this small town. You had to go to a big city like Kampala to get a professional cut.

John had finished all the pending jobs in hand. The boys who were helping him had gone home for the weekend. He took his time having a shower and then change into light cream-coloured slacks and a cotton T-shirt.

The warm weather of Gulu used to turn cool in the evening, but there was hardly any need for warm clothing. During the daytime, most of the men preferred to dress in shorts, and only in the evenings did they wear long trousers.

When John saw Carol standing at the dining table, his eyes reflected that admiration which sent her pulse racing. She knew that the years had been knocked off her today. It could be that what she was feeling was openly visible on her face. She was over fifty but almost ten years younger than John was.

"That was a lovely dinner Carol," he said when they'd finished eating. "Thank you for going to so much trouble just to make me happy!" He got up from his seat and went over to Carol, bending over to plant a kiss on her upturned face.

It was much later after their meal that husband and wife were sitting together in their room, holding hands. It had been ages since they had sat like this, looking into each other's eyes, which were saying volumes. They didn't need to open their mouths to express their feelings. But there were some cobwebs in their lives that needed to be cleared up. So for this, they had to open their mouths and blow them away.

"John, there is something I have to tell you." Carol made the first move and told him about the secret she had been keeping within, as it concerned him as well.

The look on John's face was one of such relief and happiness that he instantly cradled Carol in his arms. "That's the best news you have given me, my darling! We should hurry and start preparing to go to Kampala."

"John, have some patience. There are twelve hours between tonight and tomorrow. We'll certainly leave after breakfast in the morning." She was about to disengage herself from John's arms when he pulled her back.

"Not so soon, Carol. Just stay put. I have to give you some fantastic news now. Mine is even better than yours."

He told her the whole episode of how he had spent the night with the Indian maid who had been working in his house for nearly two years. He lowered his eyes as if to conceal his embarrassment.

"I don't know what came over me! I had always controlled myself from getting deeply involved with any woman during the time I was single. Somehow, slowly but gradually, she started to take an interest in my welfare. God knows there was sheer and lusty pleasure in holding her in my arms that night. You don't need any strong drink to get lost in the sensual pleasure of a passionate moment."

The room was silent after he stopped talking. Carol was listening to him wide-eyed, her lips parted slightly. She was visualising what John was telling her.

"Is this your bombshell, John? I was expecting some exciting news that you were so eager to give me." Carol's sarcasm was evident.

John stared into her eyes and slowly uttered, "What if I tell you that the result of that one night of passion gave us a valuable gift?" He asked it innocently, wanting to see the expression on her face.

"Which gift you are talking about, John? Why are you keeping me in suspense?" Carol was losing her patience now.

"It's strange, Carol, that the person who meant the world to you happens to be that precious gift from God."

"You don't mean ... ?"

"Yes, Carol, I mean our young Dr Vickram!"

"Is it true, John? You're not kidding?" Carol's eyes were full of unshed tears. They were tears of happiness.

How long they stayed like that! They were totally unaware of the time. Dawn had crept in slowly, and the chirping of birds could be heard. They became aware of their current situation. Quietly they went towards their bed to catch some sleep.

Guy Fawkes Night falls on every fifth of November, while Diwali is around October or November. But this time, 1972's Diwali and Guy Fawkes Night happened to fall on the same day. But what a dull time it turned out to be—no candles to light indoors and no wood fire to sit around and watch.

In spite of it being a gloomy day, everyone was trying to cheer up Vickram. The nurses were constantly coming in the room, either to check his pulse or bring Diwali presents and flowers from the hospital staff.

Nurse Alice was keeping a close watch on Vickram's progress. She had had a talk with Dr Mathews about the slow progress in his recovery. What Dr Mathews told her had made her heart weep with emotion. She was thinking that if Vickram had stopped his fiancée from going to England, she would have been near him now and he would have come out of the trauma of the after-effect of the accident. She wished there was some way to get him out of his depressed state.

She had also expressed her concern to Vickram's father. In response, he had assured Alice that he was going to see that this evening was memorable for his son. She left it at that, wondering if he must have a magic wand.

Girish Patel decided to go see if he could buy some candles and sweets from some of the shops in the main street of Kampala. He was aware that the owners of small shops had already left Kampala. There were big stores run by Uganda citizens. These stores sold everything from household accessories to groceries. He had been advised to hire a taxi in order to go around without fear of being attacked by the Kondos.

He had booked himself in a hotel that was a stone's throw from the hospital. The hotel reception had arranged for the taxi to take him around the city and look for a place where he could shop safely. There was someone else besides the driver in the taxi. One of the hospital porters wanted to do a bit of shopping as well, so Girish had some company. He was amused because he knew who had planned it. Who else other than Dr Mathews!

He was glad that Captain Hussain had arranged for Vickram's belongings to be picked up from his flat in Gulu. He was coming with his wife to join everyone this evening to celebrate Diwali. He was thinking wishfully that he had planned to celebrate this Diwali at home, with Vickram and the rest of his family. Puja had already arrived from India, and Akash was supposed to be in Nairobi today.

Thinking about his children, he decided to make a phone call later this evening. They could talk to their brother as well and wish him a happy Diwali.

What he didn't know was that Dr Kimberley and Carol were also going to be there this evening. It was kept a secret. Unaware of the events of the evening, he watched the view from the window of the car.

• The Secret of Anu •

There were hardly any shoppers walking on the pavements. There were local habitants busy in their daily routine of carrying on with their work, such as putting vegetable stalls in the market and sitting with piles of ready-made children's clothing. They were hoping that someone would still come to buy goods from them.

Girish was feeling sorry for these people, for this was clearly their daily bread. In due time, they would go back to their villages and get on with cultivating their land. It would take a while to get everything back to normal once the ninety days' deadline was over. He was thinking while getting out of the car and going towards the glass doors of the big store.

While Girish Patel was away, there was no one with Vickram during the afternoon hours. The heat at this time was making everyone a bit lazy, with the exception of the doctors and nurses who were busy with their jobs at hand.

Vickram opened his eyes and looked around. He wondered why it was so quiet there. Even the nurses seemed to have disappeared. His throat was dry, and he wanted to have a sip of cool water. He was about to press the bell when the door opened slightly and Nurse Alice peeped in.

"Hello, sir, are you all right?"

"I am glad to see you, Nurse! I was about to call you. I'm all right but slightly thirsty. It's hot in here. Could you be kind enough to get me some water, please?"

The nurse came inside the room and picked up the jug from the little side cabinet. She filled the glass with water and handed it to Vickram with a smile. "Here is cool water for you, sir. I have opened the window for the cool breeze to come in the room. You'll be all right in a little while. By the way, there is someone waiting to see you. That's why I came to see you in the first place."

"Who wants to see me apart from my father and the people of Gulu?"

"A charming young lady who says you know her. Shall I tell her to come in, sir?"

"I don't know."

"Maybe you'll feel better after you have seen her."

"There are only two women who could make me feel happy at this moment. One was my mother, who left me pining for her. The other one was the love of my life, and I sent her away! Apart from those two ladies, who else wants to see me?"

"There is still someone who wants to see you, Vickram!"

The nurse quietly left the room. Vickram was startled to hear the familiar voice. He looked towards the door. The light from the doorway revealed a silhouette coming towards him. As the black shadow came nearer to his bed, he could see the clear picture of the face that had been haunting him all this time. He thought that he must be dreaming, so he shut his eyes tightly. When he opened them again, the soul-stirring face was still there.

"Tanya!" he cried. He tried to sit up, but two hands gently pushed him back on the pillow. He was staring at her.

"You were supposed to be in England by now! I've been visualising you sitting in the plane and getting off at Heathrow Airport. Then driving to some unknown place from where you were supposed to phone me about your safe landing. I was driving back to Gulu, but my mind was with you. That's why I had this accident. A silly absent-minded Vickram sitting behind the wheels but not concentrating on his driving—this is the result! A broken collarbone and injury to the head."

For a long moment, they just stared at one another without blinking their eyes. It seemed as if time had come to a standstill.

Vickram had to make an effort to put up his hand and block her gaze. The reaction was instant. Tanya collapsed on the bed, her body rocking with heartbreaking sobs. She didn't realise that her head had hit the part of Vickram's chest where the bandage was concealing the wound. The stitches hadn't come out yet.

Vickram winced in pain but didn't utter a sound. Tanya felt him shudder and quickly lifted her head from his chest.

"I am so sorry, Vickram." Tanya's tear-stained face was staring at him. "What have you done to punish yourself like this? I should have persuaded my uncle and aunt to let me stay behind with you." She slowly and gently caressed his bandaged chest, finally resting her hand on his forehead, where the bandage was still tied.

Vickram caught her hand, and squeezing it, he murmured, "The pain has disappeared with your magic touch, my darling. Tell me, how did you manage to fly back from England so quickly?"

"That is going to be a secret for the time being. I am not allowed to spill the beans. Just think that it was a magic wand that made me appear like a flash."

"I dare say that it does look like some magic trick!" Saying this, he wrapped his arms around her neck, her locks flowing all over her face. He pushed them away to have a good look at the lovely face he had adored from the first moment he had seen her. Her eyes were half closed, her lips slightly parted.

He slowly lowered his head, and the next moment, he was holding that sweet mouth in a kiss that was full of ecstasy and longing. All the pent-up passion came to the surface. It was very quiet in the room, the only sound the beating of their hearts. It was their world alone.

It was getting dark. The lights were coming on in and around the hospital area, and the dim corridors seemed to come alive with the glare of the tube lights. Footsteps could be heard outside the room where Vickram and Tanya were locked in an embrace. They were oblivious to the rest of the world.

A knock on the door suddenly brought them to reality. Tanya took Vickram's arms away from her and placed them gently by his side.

Nurse Alice was standing in the doorway, holding a tray with tea and biscuits on it. There were some candles besides a plate of sweets. Putting the tray on the small table beside the bed, she smiled at them and said, "It is strange that I am wishing you a happy Diwali at the end of the day! Actually, Mr Girish Patel has given a treat to the hospital staff for your recovery, sir. Also for Miss Tanya's unexpected arrival ... to see you. I wish you could have seen the joy on your father's face when he was told that Miss Tanya never went away."

Vickram threw up his arms in exasperation. "Charming! Everyone knew about Tanya except me!" He turned towards the nurse. "Where is my father? I want him to meet Tanya."

"Oh, that's great, sir! I'll go find out if he is back from his hotel." She turned to go out but was surprised to see that he was already there, waiting outside. She was puzzled to see a number of people standing beside him as well. They all stopped outside and let Mr Girish Patel go inside.

"Well, I must be going, sir. It seems as if there is going to be a Diwali celebration here." She chuckled and promptly left the room.

Vickram had seen his father coming towards him. He had pulled himself up in a slightly sitting position.

"How are you, my son? Girish came up to him and kissed him on the forehead.

"I feel much better now, Papa." He stopped talking and looked at his father, who was already smiling at Tanya. "It looks as if you two have met each other!"

Girish Patel roared with laughter. "I don't believe this! My son should be introducing his fiancée to me, but instead I have the good fortune of meeting her first . . ." He stopped talking when the nurse popped her head through the door and warned them to talk in a low tone.

Vickram was about to say something, but Tanya stopped him. She had seen Dr Kimberley and Carol waiting outside the door. But the first person to enter the room was Captain Hussain, who was beaming happily when he held out his hand towards the patient and said

"Surprised to see all of us, Vickram? We couldn't wait to see you now that you're getting better." He motioned to the remaining party to join them as well.

"Captain Hussain . . . Nargis! What a lovely surprise you've all given me. Is this the Diwali gift about which the nurse was telling me?"

"Only partly, Vickram. You already have one surprise gift with you." Captain Hussain looked at Tanya and then back at the young doctor.

In reply, Vickram smiled. Looking at Tanya, he said. "Oh yeah, Captain! Tanya is the one gift I hadn't even imagined to get so soon."

"You have to thank Nargis for that, Vickram." Carol came forward, holding the pretty wife of Hussain by the arm.

"Actually, you should be thanking both husband and wife, for Captain Hussain got you out of the wreckage of your car. His driver had already taken his wife home to Gulu. Therefore, you can imagine how difficult it must have been for him to go through the ordeal single-handed."

Vickram was quiet for a while. He was holding Captain's hand and patting it. His eyes were full of gratitude. He wanted to say something, but the captain spoke first.

"Now, Vickram, don't say anything else. I was there and saw the accident right in front of my eyes. It was a good thing I had decided to keep behind because I was afraid something like that was bound to happen. After seeing Tanya off, you were walking like a zombie. I bet that if I had called out to you at that time, you wouldn't have paid any heed. Nargis is the one you should be thankful to."

"What has Nargis to do with Tanya's coming here?" Bewildered, Vickram looked at everyone assembled around him.

Nargis decided to quench his curiosity. Coming near him, she sat down on the chair so that she could explain how she had managed to get Tanya back to him.

"When you were waving your hand in farewell to Tanya, I was about to leave the airport. By chance, I spotted you when you turned back. My God, Vickram, you looked like a ghost out of a grave! My heart literally wept for you. I don't know how, but my mind came into motion and a brilliant idea came to me.

"On an impulse, I decided to go ahead with my plan. The advantage of being an army captain's wife was proving useful. I used my influence and convinced the immigration officer with a sob story. I told them that Tanya was the wife of a doctor who had fallen seriously ill. She should not be allowed to board the plane, as her presence could be required for his recovery. Within minutes, I was dragging Tanya by the arm and straight out of the airport. Luckily, her hand luggage was still with her. The rest of it was well on its way to the UK."

"Hussain had already instructed the driver to take us back to Gulu before it got really dark. To cut the story short, I took Tanya back with me. It took her a while to understand my motive. I had to take somebody in my confidence, and who was better than Carol! She was so excited when I told her that Tanya was with me, and she wanted to take her home. She thought Tanya would feel more at home if she was in the Kimberley household."

Vickram suddenly found his voice. "I don't get it. Why did you keep Tanya with you when you came to know about my accident? All the time I was here, didn't she want to see me even once? How is that possible?"

Hussain spoke before his wife could say anything. "You're right, Vickram. I had instructed Nargis to keep the news about the accident away from Tanya's ears. It was only yesterday, when Dr Kimberley told us that they were planning to give Vickram a surprise gift for Diwali, that we decided we should take Tanya to see you. I felt guilty for keeping her in the dark about your accident, because after hearing what had happened to you, Tanya really went berserk."

Everyone present in the room had to say something. Girish Patel was amused but happy that his son had been living amongst such kind and friendly people. They seemed like a big family.

Dr Kimberley was having a quiet talk with Girish. No one could hear what was being said, but after a while, Dr Kimberley got up from his seat.

"Listen, all of you. I am going to see if Dr Mathew is in his room He wanted to see both Vickram and Tanya together. I won't be long."

Everyone stopped talking. They were looking at the door after Dr Kimberley made his exit. Before they could resume their talk, Dr Mathews walked in.

"Hello, everybody! It's nice to see such rejoicing going on during these troubled times. How are you feeling now, young man?" After addressing Vickram, he then looked at Tanya and held out his hand to greet her. "So you are Tanya, the remedy for Vickram's quick recovery! I am very thankful to Captain Hussain and his wife for their foresight in bringing you two together again."

"I am also extremely thankful to you, Dr Mathews, for treating me as a priority case. I am going to remember your kind gesture when I return home to Nairobi. I hope that one day you might come for a safari holiday in Kenya. You won't be able to resist the offer, sir!" Vickram's voice was full of compassion.

"Well, young man, thanks for the invitation. I am sure that I may be able to make it to Kenya before all of you leave for the UK. Anyway, we don't know what awaits us round the corner. After all, it's destiny that decides our future." He looked closely at Vickram and said, "Actually, Vickram . . ." He paused and looked around the room at everyone. Then he said, "I want to talk to Vickram alone. This won't take long."

Everybody left one by one, and within a short time, the room was empty. Even Tanya had had to follow the rest of the party. Dr Mathews looked at the door and quietly closed it.

Vickram looked questioningly at him. He smiled and brought his chair near to Vickram. He started talking slowly.

"Relax, Vickram! There is something important I have to tell you. I couldn't say anything with everybody present here."

Vickram became worried and asked quickly, "Is it something to do with my accident, sir?"

"No, Vickram. Not really! As far as your well-being is concerned, you are okay and going towards a quick recovery. I wanted to tell you that due to your head injury, you lost a lot of blood. We needed more blood to carry out your operation of your cracked collarbone. It was very frustrating to find that the blood bank didn't have the right type of blood. We had to inform Dr Kimberley, just in case he could find the matching blood group in one of the hospitals in Gulu.

"We wanted Mr Girish Patel to take the next flight because as your father, he was the best person to give his blood. But I was shocked when he told me on the phone that his blood wouldn't match." He paused and waited for Vickram to say something, but the young doctor was quiet.

"I'm going to give you a shock because that's what I got when he told me that he wasn't your father!"

Vickram opened his mouth then. "So now even you know he's not my father. You don't have any inclination what agony I went through when I found out the truth about my birth! My dying mother's last words told me that my biological father was an English doctor." His voice held so much bitterness in it that Dr Mathews wondered whether he should continue with this conversation any further.

"Tell me, Vickram, do you really want to find out about this doctor?"

"I honestly have no idea how I am going to react if he suddenly comes in front of me."

"After your operation, in your delirious state; you had been mumbling quite a lot. I had gathered that there were a lot of questions on your mind. You wanted answers but got none."

"You are right, Doctor. I wanted to know about the man who had taken my identity away from me! One minute I was the happy-go-lucky son of Mr Girish Patel. And the next minute, I became someone who didn't have a father! I went berserk at first but then decided to find out about the mysterious doctor.

"Even while I was carrying out my work at the hospital, I was busy collecting all the information regarding those doctors who had been working in Nairobi in nineteen thirty-nine. Luckily, I did manage to find out something from the hospital records in Kampala. But bad luck here as well because the doctor whose details matched with the description I had in hand had unfortunately gone back to England. I felt so disheartened and wretched that I decided to go back to Kenya, but the MO of Mulago Hospital offered me the job at Lacor Hospital in Gulu."

"Well, I had gathered something like this. But have you given up your quest, Vickram?"

"What does it matter, sir! I am still in the dark. For the last three to four years, I have tried my best to solve this mystery. It seems as if my quest will remain unfulfilled."

"Don't give up so soon, for what I am going to tell you will ease that burden from your mind. For you see, whoever gave the right type of blood for the operation didn't come forward personally. Our nurse Alice revealed the name of the mystery person whose blood matched with yours. I am going to give you another shock! I sent the blood sample of both of you for a DNA test. My suspicion was confirmed. The mystery donor is your biological father."

Vickram sat up straight. His face had become blank. He stared at the doctor and tried to digest what had been said to him. Then all of a sudden, he became excited. He grabbed the wrist of Dr Mathews. Shaking it, he blurted out, "Please tell me who this person is, sir. Does he know about me? Is he from somewhere in Kampala? You just tell me his name. I am not sure if I'll be able to control my anger if I see him in person."

"No, Vickram, I won't tell you his name yet. You have to get better soon. Once you are out of the hospital and feeling one hundred per cent fit, only then I will take you personally to him or bring him over to see you."

Dr Mathews watched the look of disappointment shadowing the excitement that was on Vickram's face earlier. He felt sorry for the young doctor, but he was determined that there should not be too much excitement, for it might hinder the swift recovery of his patient. Seeing Tanya today unexpectedly was enough for him to digest for the time being.

Before he called the rest of the party to come back in the room, Dr Mathews turned back and said, "By the way,

Vickram, tomorrow your stitches are going to come out. If the healing process is normal, then you'll hopefully be discharged soon." He was hardly out of the door when Tanya and the rest of the party promptly swarmed around the young doctor.

Girish Patel sat in one corner, his face beaming. "I never thought that God would be so kind to shower a rain of happiness on us! I have got my son back with a bonus in the form of a charming daughter-in-law."

"She is not your daughter-in-law yet, Papa. Not until we tie the matrimonial knot."

"Oh, don't worry about that, my son! As soon as we arrive in Nairobi, I am going to start making all the preparations for your wedding and a lavish reception afterwards."

They all left one by one, as it was getting late and it was time for Vickram's rest. Tanya stayed a bit longer with him. She didn't have to go with Nargis now, as Girish had booked extra rooms in the hotel where he was staying. He knew that after Vickram was discharged from the hospital, they'd have to stay here a bit longer. It was a special request by Dr Mathews.

Dr Kimberley and Carol had asked him to come over and stay with them when Vickram was discharged, but were refused because Captain Hussain pointed out that the checkpoints on the way to Gulu were still in operation. They had all accepted Girish Patel's invitation of a dinner at the hotel after Vickram left the hospital.

Chapter 17

Two days after the Diwali and Guy Fawkes Day, Vickram was discharged from the hospital in the morning. He was told to take it easy for the first few days. His father had made sure that the room he had been given by the hotel manager was comfortable, with extra furniture for his needs. A lovely lounger was put near the window. He could lie down and look out at the lovely view of colourful flowers in the hospital gardens. There was a water fountain in the middle of the green lawn. He could also see the vast structure of part of the hospital.

After talking with the hotel manager, Girish phoned Captain Hussain and Dr Kimberley with the invitation for dinner in the hotel's restaurant. They accepted the invitation eagerly, as they wanted to see Vickram out of the hospital robe.

Dr Mathews and Alice, the nurse, were the first ones to arrive. They told Mr Girish Patel to go see if Vickram was ready while they sat and waited for the others.

Tanya was already waiting for the guests before she decided to go and see if Vickram was ready. She knocked on the door softly and opened it to peep in. "Wow, Vickram! You look like a million dollars. Gosh, I've never seen you dressed like this before. Your hairstyle and this velvet jacket . . . I'm glad there is no other female around to challenge me."

She was staring at this complete changeover in Vickram's appearance. His hair was trimmed and styled, with a golden shine to his brown locks. The parting in the middle gave a slight rise to the sides, which were shaped in a slightly curly style. The freshly shaven face looked so soft and appealing that she felt like caressing his cheeks softly with her own. His eyes looked less haunted than before, but that sadness was still lurking somewhere in the corners of his eyes.

She moved towards him with an adorable look in her eyes, and he reached for her. In an instant, she was crushed against him. She felt such a surge of compassion for her beloved that she placed her head on his chest.

Vickram lifted her face up to look properly at her. The memory of this face had been haunting him the entire time he was in the hospital. He was regretting the moment when he had let her go with her uncle and aunt. If he had stopped her, then all this drama would not have happened.

• THE SECRET OF ANU •

He kept his hold on her, forgetting where they were. His gaze was fixed on her eyes; the sparkle was back in them. He also realised that her thick curly hair had gone. The straight shining hair was brushed in long locks that gave her a mature look. The simple style brought out the lovely shape of her oval face and gave a mysterious look to her big almond-shaped eyes.

He brushed away the fringe that kept coming over her eyes. "Why didn't you cut this curly fringe as well while changing your hairstyle?"

"Because, darling, you used to love playing with this fringe, so how could I get rid of something you liked so much?"

They were not aware that Girish Patel was watching them. He had come to tell Vickram that the rest of the party wanted to come and spend some time with him. There was plenty of time to kill before dinner. He saw that the door was partly open and slowly touched it with his knuckle.

Hearing the knock, they quickly separated. Tanya's cheeks were red. "Sorry, Uncle!"

"Sorry for what, my dear? Seeing you two together like this gives me immense pleasure. By the way, did you notice Vickram's new hairstyle?"

"Oh yes! I was wondering who could have helped him."

"This hotel has excellent service. The hotel manager sent a good hairdresser to help Vickram. He needed a good shave to get rid of all that stubble that had gone haywire."

Vickram chuckled. "You two make me feel like an exhibition piece. Anyway, when are the rest of our guests going to come?"

Captain Hussain's cheerful voice came from the doorway. "We're here, Dr Vickram! We have been here for a while. Your father asked us to come a bit early so that we have some spare time to have a good chat before going to the restaurant."

He came up to the young doctor and shook his hand in greeting. He was quite tall and big, overshadowing everyone in the room. Today he was looking slightly different. It could be because he was not wearing his uniform. Nargis was by his side, holding on to his hand.

Vickram stared at her and thought that she still had that charm and beauty that could captivate any man. He thanked God that he came out of his trance quickly before Hassan could get any wind of it.

Nargis came up to him and shook his hand as if he were a stranger, knowing very well that Hussain's hawk-like gaze was on her every movement. It was a fact that Hussain was very possessive about his beautiful wife.

"Why is Dr Kimberley late, Nargis?" Tanya asked her while looking at the door. "I thought you were coming together."

"That's what I was expecting, Tanya, because they left an hour earlier than us. I hope they haven't gotten into any trouble with the men from the force at the checkpoints!" Nargis looked worried.

• The Secret of Anu •

Girish Patel looked at his watch. "I think they could be waiting in the lobby. Dr Kimberley rang earlier on that there was something important he wanted to ask Dr Mathews. Let me ring the reception desk and find out." He went to pick up the receiver and was about to dial the number when there was a sudden commotion outside the room. He hung up the phone because he heard the sound of laughter coming nearer to them.

The next minute, the door opened. Dr Mathews was sharing a joke with Carol, who was having a bout of laughter, tears flowing from her eyes. Nurse Alice was also laughing, but she had control of herself, unlike Carol.

"I bet Dr Mathews has been telling one of his jokes,." Vickram said, looking at the coming party.

"Oh! Sorry for being a bit naughty, Vickram!" Carol said apologetically, giving him a motherly cuddle. "You don't know how happy I feel to see you back on your feet! You couldn't even imagine the agony we went through when we saw you at the hospital with those injuries. Now I feel that both of my children are back with me." She turned towards Tanya to give her a cuddle as well. Her eyes were moist. No one could have imagined that at the time, she was telling the truth. Only Dr Mathews knew what she meant.

Vickram looked around as if his eyes were searching for someone. Dr Mathews noticed that and decided to let the final curtain come down now.

"So, Vickram, as I promised you, now that you are well on the road to recovery, I'll introduce you to the person you have been looking for over the last four years. At last, your quest is going to be over!"

He made the surprise announcement and gestured to someone who was standing outside the door to come forward. When Dr Kimberley walked in, there was dead silence. Dr Mathews went forward and shook hands with him.

"Welcome, Dr Kimberley. There is someone who is dying to meet his biological father."

Dr Kimberley's eyes were moist when he walked towards Vickram. He had been waiting for this moment ever since he came to know that he did have a son of his own. He was not childless. There was someone to carry on the Kimberley name after him.

Nothing could describe the inner joy and ecstasy of this moment. There was no word to describe what Vickram felt then! He looked at the person who had always been so near to him. He couldn't digest the fact that the unknown person, his biological father, had been with him all this time. Knowing Dr Kimberley made it difficult to believe that he could have left his mother alone in the big wide world!

He knew that something had pulled him towards Gulu, and he had always wondered what it could have been. Perhaps the blood bond was so strong that it was pulling him towards his goal. The father he had been searching for was so near him, and he never knew. Was this another of nature's amazing tricks? Only God knew about it.

• The Secret of Anu •

There was not a word spoken for a long moment—only the sheer magic of a father and son's embrace! That told everyone what a blood relationship meant: love in abundance, which both Carol and John felt for Vickram at that moment.

It was much later, when they were coming out of the restaurant, that Vickram found his voice in order to address Dr Kimberley about what he had been wondering. "I can't understand, Dad . . . When we were going through the hospital records, all we came across was the name of Dr Nicholas with a blurred surname that couldn't be read. Some spill of water had washed the letters, leaving only an impression of blue ink."

"You did find the right person, Vickram, because my full name is John Nicholas Kimberley. My father was called Nicholas Gerald Kimberley. Gerald was my grandfather's name. But after his death, I shortened my name when I had to renew my passport before coming back to Uganda."

"But the records of the old Kampala hospital showed that Dr Nicholas went back to England."

"That's right, son, for I did go back, but I returned to take my post of a senior doctor at Lacor Hospital in Gulu."

"Aha, that explains it all!" Vickram said with satisfaction.

Carol had been quiet all this time. Now she looked at Vickram and said, "You were so quiet and aloof in the beginning, Vickram. I wish you had opened up a bit and talked to us about all that was in your heart. Why couldn't you confide in us?"

"Because I had this notion within me that it was my mother's secret and no one should even know about it."

"Ah, yes, Vickram. It was Anu's secret after all!" Girish had been very quiet, and the sudden outburst from him made the others stop in their tracks.

Dr Kimberley remembered something suddenly and looked at Vickram and Tanya. "I am so sorry, Tanya, that in our excitement, I totally forgot to mention a call from England. Bobby phoned yesterday just as I came home. They are in one of the army camps, waiting for their resettlement. I also told Bobby to tell Deepak that his niece is in safe hands and that soon you and Vickram will be coming over to England to get their blessings."

It made Tanya happy to know that her uncle and aunt had gotten the message about her safety. She looked up and thanked God.

Vickram's quest was over. It was left to Girish Patel and Dr Kimberley to decide where the wedding would take place. Tanya wouldn't have dreamed that her marriage to Vickram, which had seemed to be on a distant horizon, was at last it becoming a reality ... and so soon!

Dr Kimberley turned towards Girish. "Well, Mr Patel, when you arrive in Nairobi and start making preparations for the wedding, I will arrange for my annual leave. I was actually planning to take this leave during Christmastime, but destiny always has different plans for us. I know it's going to be a bit difficult to leave the hospital, as there is already a shortage of doctors. I am sure there will be some doctor to take over the charge of running the hospital in my absence."

In the end, it was decided that John and Carol would come to Nairobi only a day earlier than the wedding day. They wanted to spend the rest of their holiday sightseeing in Nairobi. Then, if the political situation in Uganda didn't improve, they'd fly to the UK.

Girish was thoughtful and came out with what he had been thinking. "In that case, Dr Kimberley, I'll also send Vickram and Tanya to England. I am sure that because you're his real father, Vickram won't need a visa now to enter Britain."

Tanya jumped with joy. "It's a fantastic idea, Uncle! We'll be able to see our folks over there. My aunt and uncle will be able to give their blessings which they could have given on our wedding day."

Vickram was quick to join in. "Of course, Tanya. Maybe one day we might find our feet firmly planted on the British soil. Then Papa could come there as well, with Puja and Akaash."

"Don't forget, Vickram. If there is a chance for you to carry on studying further—I mean, to accomplish your ambition to become a fully qualified paediatrician—then by all means, go ahead! I'll willingly support you financially."

Vickram held his papa in a tight embrace. His voice was full of compassion for this man. "I am the luckiest of all the sons who has two fathers to call Papa and Dad!"

Their laughter filled the hotel corridors, spreading a feeling of happiness all around. Dr Mathews had the last word. "Well, Vickram, I had expected a shower of angry rainfall pouring down on poor Dr Kimberley!"

Vickram looked at his newly discovered dad with a sheepish grin.

ABOUT THE AUTHOR

R. K. Dogra is a Punjabi short-story writer. She has been writing short stories and articles for Punjabi magazines and weeklies for the past twenty years or so.

She had a sudden attack of rheumatoid arthritis and was advised to take an early retirement from her last job, which was with Ealing Council. In spite of working full time, she also enjoyed looking after her grandchildren. Once they were ready to attend school full time, she realised that it was time for her to do something creative.

In the past years, while working outside her home, she managed to get a number of stories published in the Punjabi papers and the monthly magazine. Once she had time on her hands, she decided to get them published in book form. Her second book was published a few years ago.

Her popularity as a writer for women gave her many opportunities to air her views on Desi Radio, most notably on March 8, when celebrating Women's Day.

She had the gift of becoming a fine arts graduate, but early hardships in life made that task impossible. Coming to England was a bonus and allowed her to fulfill her ambitions. She joined the correspondence school ICS and achieved a diploma in portrait painting in oils.

Her love for reading books in English and Punjabi stirred up a wish to write something in English. The chance came when her granddaughter suggested that it would be nice if she wrote something about her early life, which she spent in Kenya and Uganda.

The suggestion gave her an idea to write a novel based on the life she had to face with her family upon Amin's order of expulsion of all Asians from Uganda in 1972. She had so many ideas that she had to give herself a deadline of ninety days.

This novel, The Secret of Anu, is the first attempt by the author to write in English. It is a historical novel, and she hopes that readers will overlook any flaws in expression and dialect.